I0730956

THIS IS WHERE I SLEEP

TIFFANY PATTERSON

PROLOGUE

2 011

CORAL

Like shards of broken glass scraping my insides. So this is what a broken heart feels like.

I've wondered.

Now I know as I read the letter in my hands.

DEAR CECE,

I can't do this.

Li

THAT'S IT. *Three lines. That's all he left me with. The one person I trusted with my whole heart and soul. The one who knew me inside and out, knew my deepest fears, and promised he'd never leave me.*

My best friend.

He left anyway.

Was this a dream? I hoped it was just a dream, a figment of my imagination. I'd wake up and Li would still be here. But I knew it was not a dream. The stickiness between my thighs told me that I hadn't imagined all the things we'd done last night and well into the morning. The reddish-purple half-moon shaped marks on my breasts and inner thighs were further proof that Li was here. And the wetness that dripped from my cheeks onto the paper gripped tightly in my hand further confirmed this wasn't a dream. After all the shit I'd been through, this moment right here is my worst nightmare.

Li was gone.

The finality in his note told me he was not coming back.

I laid back on the bed and let the painful realization consume me whole.

I hated hospitals.

The incessant beeping of the heart-rate monitor had me ready to toss it out of the eighth floor window. The barren nature of these rooms brought back too many memories of being nine years old and seeing my mother laying in a hospital bed surrounded by nothing but white, sterile walls.

I hated it.

"You want to watch the news?" my cousin Quincy asked.

I sighed and looked over at him. He was the only person that helped me hold it together. He was still pissed at me for not letting him tell the rest of the family that I was here in the hospital, but I didn't need their sympathy or their questions.

I shrugged and pushed my hands through shoulder-length relaxed hair, which was a matted, unruly mess from my days' long hospital stay.

"Yeah, sure," I responded to Quincy's offer. He turned on CNN and the coverage was of some American arrested in Iran for hiking. Both Quincy and I grunted at that, knowing damn well hiking was code word for spying. America would deny it though.

"I bet she was hiking. And leaving a damn trail for the rest..." Quincy began.

This was safe territory for us. I half listened as he talked about weapons of mass destruction and warheads that may or may not be in Iran. I was sick of hearing about all that shit. I'd fought enough battles over those wars. Unfortunately, this discussion did bring up a decision I needed to make regarding one of two choices for my career. I could complete my contract with the Army for the next two years, or take the other offer, which would let me out of serving my final two years; but it would have me changing hands from one government entity to another...an entity that was an even deeper one than my current position.

"And in business and political news, the son of billionaire oil tycoon, Richard Bennett of Texas is engaged..."

My head snapped to the flat screen television mounted on the hospital wall as the reporter continued to fill the viewing audience in on the engagement between one Michele Price and Liam Bennett, or as I called him, Li.

He was my former best friend and the man that I was in love with.

I heard my own heart beating wildly in my chest. I blinked away unshed tears as images of Li's six-foot-three frame, draped in a perfectly tailored dark blue suit stood beside the perfect blonde who proudly displayed what looked to be a three-karat Tiffany diamond on her left hand. She was dressed in a white floral dress as if practicing for the big day already. She looked like a beauty queen poised next to Li. And she didn't just look the part of a beauty queen; she actually was a beauty queen—Miss Texas in 2005. She was Li's ex, the one who was so perfect at everything that it made my teeth itch.

When Li turned his emerald eyes on her and placed a kiss on her rose colored lips, I gripped my abdomen from the physical pain that his display of affection caused.

"That motherfucker," I heard Quincy growl at the same time he pointed the remote to turned off the TV,

"No, Quincy! Don't!" I yelled. I needed to see it. I needed the images burned into my brain, to remember why I was where I was, while Li had just announced to the world that he was engaged to someone else only weeks after telling me I was the love of his life.

I felt the sharp edges of my broken heart again. I had been numb since that initial night. Now, the pain had returned tenfold. But I didn't cry. Not this time. Instead, Li's decision forced me to make a decision of my own. Since he had decided to move on with his life, it was time for me to do the same. I took one last look at the screen to remember the heavy weight in my chest and the feeling of betrayal.

"Hand me the phone," I said to Quincy.

His dark, questioning brown eyes turned to mine. "Coral, you can't call him. He—"

"Fuck him. This has nothing to do with him, Quince. I need to make a phone call in private." It was a partial lie. While I wasn't calling Li, in truth, I'd already tried a few times but his numbers were all disconnected. The call that I was making was about my future. "Quince, the phone," I repeated when he just looks at me. He met my glare with a dark scowl that might've intimidated others, but not me.

Finally, he relented and handed me the phone as I asked.

"I need some privacy," I reiterated, picking up the receiver.

He nodded and stood to leave. "I'll be back in the morning," he said before strolling out of the room.

I won't be here, I thought, as I watched him walk out the door. Picking up my clothing from the chair on the side of my bed, I flipped through my wallet until I found the card I was looking for. I dialed the number without giving it a second thought.

"Yeah," a deep, gravelly voice answered.

"I'm in."

"You're in? Just like that?" he asked, skeptically.

I sighed. "I said I'm in. You've spent months trying to recruit me. I know you still want me. I said I'm in."

"You know there's no take-backs. No do-overs," he advised. "Once you're in, you're in."

His words gave me pause. Was this the life I wanted? My eyes shifted back to the TV screen where another image of Li and his new fiancé was displayed. This time it was a picture of them on a beach in Cabo. It was a few years old. The camera then flashed to present day image, zooming in on the sparkling rock on Michele's finger.

"I'm in."

"Okay, I'll be by in a few hours to pick you up."

"I'm not home. I'm—"

"At Memorial Health, room 811," he said, finishing my sentence.

I should have known he'd know where I was.

"I'll be ready," I said.

After looking at the screen one last time, I flicked the power button on the remote and the screen went dark.

"Goodbye, Li," I mumbled before standing to pack my things. It was clear that the chapter of Liam and I was over. That's life. It had never been too kind to me before, why start now?

CHAPTER 1

resent Day
Coral

I turned left off the dirt road, deep in the Virginia woods to see the small cabin I'd been expecting to see. I slowed down to a creep, sure that as soon as I entered the property there would be guns trained on my rented sedan. I knew my every movement was being watched on video feeds. I would've expected nothing less. This was not a social call. I was there to get much-needed information.

I pulled up a few feet away from the cabin's rear entrance, and then shut off the ignition as I had been instructed to do. Moving slowly as to not cause alarm, I opened the door and exited, holding my hands up to show I only had my key in them. Of course, my piece was tucked in my back, which I was sure they were aware of. I looked from left to right to take in my surroundings. I didn't see any movement, but I wasn't too worried. Once I approached the cabin's door, I tapped a few times with my steel toe boots. A few seconds later I was staring into a pair of dark, soulless eyes.

"You're late," he grunted.

I looked down at my wrist to find that it was a few minutes after one. I wasn't even five minutes late.

I raised an eyebrow. "It's not like this is the easiest place to find."

"Whatever, venga," he said, stepping aside to wave me in.

I entered the cabin and was immediately met with a familiar smell. It was a mixture of blood, urine and…fear.

"Has he been cooperative?" I asked.

Dark Eyes gave a sinister grin that would have made a lesser person shiver. "He's been quite cooperative since we came to a mutual understanding," he said, cracking the knuckles of his beefy hands for emphasis.

"I bet," I mumbled, shifting my gaze to take in the rest of the cabin. There wasn't much in the room besides a small wooden table with two chairs and a small television, perched on a window ledge. Towards the back of the room there was a hallway that had two doors on either side. I assumed one was the bathroom and the other a bedroom.

"Which one is he in?" I asked, nodding towards the back rooms.

"The right. You've got ten minutes to get what you need," he curtly said before moving towards the table to sit down.

"I doubt I'll need that much."

I quickly moved towards the door on the right, wanting to get this over with and be on my way. I was hoping this meeting would provide me with the answers I'd been seeking for close to two years.

I opened the door and the smell grew even more potent. It no longer turned my stomach when I saw the battered man in the bath tub. *Of course,* I thought to myself. *Easier to clean up the mess when they're done.*

His once golden skin was littered with purple and blue bruises. His right eye was swollen shut, and his nose was bleeding and broken. He'd been stripped down to a pair of boxers that were soiled with blood and urine. His left leg was contorted in a way that was unnatural. One look at this guy and I knew he'd been through the ringer. If the visual wasn't enough, the low moans of agony coming from his throat told the tale of his pain. It was almost enough to make me feel sorry for him.

Almost.

But I knew this guy was far from innocent. He'd been a notorious sex-trafficking ringleader in Central America for years. I'd spent months trying to track his elusive ass down. I also saw pictures of, and spoke with some of the young girls and women abducted on his orders, then tortured and sold off into a life of hell. So, this slime got no sympathy from me.

"What's the matter, Emilio? Not feeling well?" I whispered into his ear.

His one good eye popped open. The fear was evident.

"Por favor! Ayúdame!"

I squatted down next to the edge of the tub. "I'm not here to help you. But you're going to help me."

"Who are you?" he queried.

"Just call me Scorpion." His good eye widened in shock when I gave my name. "But my name isn't important. You have information I need. Who's your Bogota supplier?"

I got straight to the point. I studied his facial reactions carefully for the answer to my question. The bruising and beating he had taken could make it difficult to read his micro expressions as clearly as I was usually able to. Still, I was able to make out a slight rise of his eyebrows, and parting of his lips. The look lasted for less than half a second before he covered it up. Most people missed the micro expressions. Not me. I registered the look as surprise. He wasn't expecting my question. The next look I saw was fear. That look told me that he knew something.

"Come on, Emilio. I know you know what I'm talking about. I've already talked to a former employee of yours who said you get your drugs out of Colombia. Give me a name." It really wasn't an employee of his. It was actually a former trafficked girl, who was part of a ring my team had broken up a while back. When I asked for information on Emilio's partners she was eager to share what she knew.

He dismissively turned his face away from me. "No sé nada."

I leaped up and extended my left leg into the tub. "You don't know anything, huh?!" I stomped down on his awkwardly contorted leg.

"Please! Please!" he screamed in agony.

"Please *what*? You ready to talk now?"

"Okay, okay," he vigorously nodded.

I removed my foot. "Talk."

"I d-don't know much. I've never seen or spoken with him directly."

I nodded. "What's his name?"

"I don't know his name. Not a real name. I just know what everyone calls him."

"Come on, Emilio," I demanded, growing impatient.

"He's hard to track down. No one even knows what he looks like. Some say he's not even from Bogotá, but from America."

That was a bit of a shocker, but I didn't let Emilio see my surprise. "Name."

"They call him Ghost. That's all I know. I swear."

I looked at his face and knew he was telling the truth. Hearing he might be American was a surprise I wasn't expecting, but maybe I should have been. This was another piece to a puzzle I'd been trying to put together for a long time.

"Thank you, Emilio. You have truly been helpful." My tone was laced with mocking sarcasm. I stood and moved towards the door.

"Wait! Please! They're going to kill me. You have to help me!"

Before slipping out the door, I turned and gave Emilio the same answer he had given me earlier. "No sé nada."

I shut the door behind me. "He's all yours!" I called to the man still sitting at the wooden table.

"You get what you need?"

"Yeah. You guys softened him up for me. You know anyone named 'Ghost' working out of Colombia?"

His dark eyes pondered for a few seconds before he shook his head. That response wasn't surprising. He was Mexican and worked for the government. Despite our current location, this guy was actually on the side of good. He wouldn't be tied up with any drug lords.

"You will tell Mr. Salazar you were accommodated as he asked, yes?"

I nodded. "I will as soon as I see him later tonight."

"Good. What do you have against this Ghost anyway?"

I tossed the words, "He tried to kill me," over my shoulder before strolling out the door and back to my vehicle.

* * *

I SAT BACK on the king-sized bed as I heard the shower in the bathroom turn on. I'd rented a suite at the Marriott for the evening. As my guest finished showering after the workout we just had, I lay on the crumpled sheets in my robe, and thought back to what I learned earlier in the day. What Emilio revealed in that tiny cabin hadn't been much, but at least I had a name to begin asking around about. What I'd said back at the cabin was true. Ghost, whoever he was, had tried to kill me in Bogotá. Unfortunately for him, he missed. Usually, I didn't take someone trying to kill me personally.

It was the nature of what I do, or at least what I used to do. But instead of simply missing his mark, this Ghost killed two of my team members. Two people who were under my charge never made it home. *That,* I did take that personally. And I wouldn't rest until I got payback.

Not only did I need retribution for my former team, but I felt like I had a target on my back ever since. Even though I now worked with my two cousins in our own security and consulting business, I still couldn't shake the shadow of my past. I knew someone from my former life had it out for me, and that made everyone around me a potential target. It was the reason I kept my distance from my family.

I was rarely in Savannah, Georgia where our home base was. I couldn't remember the last time I had spent more than a few days with my sister in Atlanta. I was constantly working, either on cases with our firm or traveling to South America looking for answers. I hadn't told my cousins about what happened in Bogotá, nor did I plan to. I knew they'd want to help, and that would make them even more of a target. So instead, I kept my distance.

I pushed out a heavy sigh.

"What are you thinking about?" a deep, baritone voice asked from the bathroom doorway.

I was so deep in thought I hadn't noticed the shower turn off, or him standing there watching me. I looked over at six feet of beautifully sculpted muscle, encased in light caramel skin. A white towel was wrapped around his waist. I moved up his frame to find light hazel-green eyes staring back at me. The man had the whole Michael Ealy vibe happening.

"I was wondering how long it would be before you got your ass out of my shower."

He chuckled. "Oh, if that's what you were thinking about, I must have some work to do. I'm not sure I put it down well enough earlier."

He smiled down at me as he reached the bed and pulled me up by my upper arms. At my full height, the top of my head reached the top of his chest.

I smiled back as his lips hovered a few inches from mine. "No, Senator Roberts. You definitely put it down earlier."

"Have I told you how much I like it when you use my official title?" Those hazel eyes were swimming with mirth and a small amount of mischief. He placed a quick peck on my lips then moved lower to my neck.

"Mmm, as good as that feels, I have to shower and get ready and you need to head out," I said, pressing my hand to his firm chest, halting his movements.

He sighed and stood to his full height, peering down at me. I knew what he was going to say before the words came out of his mouth. I bit the inside of my cheek to keep from cutting him off.

"We could have just gone to this damn thing together." There was hint of irritation in his voice.

"We've been over this," I said, moving out of his embrace and stepping around him.

"Then let's go over it again. Why can't you be my escort to the USO Gala tonight?"

I rolled my eyes before turning back to him because I didn't feel like getting into this discussion again. "You know why not," I responded.

What we had was casual. At least that's what I thought. We saw each other when convenient, had great sex and left it at that. Public appearances weren't a part of the deal. Not to mention, an event like the USO Gala would cause all types of talk. Nathaniel Roberts was the youngest Senator in the U.S. Senate, representing the great state of Massachusetts. He was extremely popular in his home state and making waves in Washington, and had good looks to boot.

He had made the top of almost every 'most eligible bachelor' list there was. His political astuteness had many talking about him running for President in another five to ten years. He was already being touted as the next Barack Obama. The only thing missing was the wife and perfect family. But, I was nobody's Michelle.

"Right, I know why. You don't do relationships. But maybe that's bullshit. Maybe you're just scared."

Very little in this world scared me. I looked death in the face too many times to be intimidated by much, but I merely scoffed at his statement.

"When we started this, we agreed that this wasn't anything serious. Why are you trying to change that now?" I asked, my impatience growing.

"Maybe I want more now. Maybe I want to change our agreement."

I shook my head. "That's not possible."

"Why not?"

"Because I'm not the woman you marry and have the two point five kids with. I'm not the woman you run for office with at your side, smiling and waving for the cameras. It's not who I am."

"Then who are you?" he challenged.

I smiled mischievously and strolled over to him, lifting on tiptoes to put my arms around his neck. "I'm the woman you fuck until the right one comes along," I said, looking up into his eyes. I took a nip of his bottom lip before releasing my hold and stepping back to head to the bathroom to shower, but I was stopped by his grip around my waist.

"We'll see," he said before pressing a kiss to my lips and a smack to my firm ass.

I smirked and shook my head. There were times I wished I could be *that* woman. There was a time I thought my life could be different, but not anymore. Nathaniel was a great guy. I'd known him since my days in the Army. He would undoubtedly become President someday with his charm, superb intellect, and political savvy. I just wouldn't be the woman on his arm when he got there.

I rolled my eyes as he began to get dressed. I turned and headed for the shower not glancing back. I made sure to make it nice and long to ensure he'd be gone by the time I came out. I'd had enough company for one day and needed to get prepared for the gala. I usually hated attending those types of events, but since I was former military and I was formally invited by one of my clients who was a member of Congress, I couldn't turn it down.

Here goes nothing, I sighed as I stepped out of the shower and began to get ready for the evening.

CHAPTER 2

*C*oral

I stepped out of the town car and I didn't miss the chauffeur's raised brows in appreciation. I turned my head to hide my smile. I knew the long, form-fitting red sleeveless gown I was wearing fit all my curves perfectly. The slit up to the midpoint of my thigh was enough to show off my mocha-colored, toned legs. The five-inch leopard print heels added a bit of sass to my look. I ran my fingers through my curly, tapered cut and tucked my clutch under my arm before moving to the side to allow the driver to close the door.

I looked up to see the huge marquee with the U.S. flag and the words "USO GALA" in big bold letters at the entrance to the convention center. I noticed some of the nation's top business and political leaders entering to honor the men and women who serve this nation. Although I wasn't necessarily looking forward to this event, I was looking forward to seeing some comrades I hadn't seen since I'd been out of uniform.

"Oh, Coral. I'm so glad to have caught you before you went in. Allow me."

I tipped my head at Excellency Salazar from Mexico. "Your Excellency, thank you," I said, wrapping my hand around the older man's arm. In my heels, I stood a few inches above his five-foot eight inch frame.

Salazar was the Mexican official who had arranged my little rendezvous with Emilio earlier in the day. It came as a debt of gratitude for helping locate his granddaughter who had been kidnapped earlier in the year.

"I trust everything went well today, yes?"

I pondered as we entered the Convention Center. "You trust correctly, Your Excellency. I got what I was looking for."

"Excellent. I must say, Coral, you are looking lovely in that dress. If I were twenty years younger…"

"You would still be married with five kids." We both laughed at my comeback. I looked around for his wife. "Where is Señora Salazar, by the way?"

We both knew Mr. Salazar, while being a seemingly doting husband, could also become a little touchy feely when he'd had too much to drink, and the drinks would be flowing soon.

"She will be along shortly…"

He continued talking as we made our way further inside the gala, but an odd sensation had me tuning out his words. The hairs on the back of my neck stood up and a chill ran down my spine. I knew the feeling. It'd been a long time since I'd sensed it, but I knew it, and only one person had ever brought out the odd sensation. Someone I hadn't seen in five years.

I looked up and turned my head to the left, casually looking around. That slight movement had me locking eyes with a pair of emerald eyes that for the last half a decade, I had only seen in my dreams. *Liam.* His expression was unreadable. He was one of the only people I couldn't read easily. He simply stared at me. He made no effort to acknowledge my presence or come over to me.

That pain I'd buried in the pit of my stomach five years ago threatened to emerge and bubble over. My throat went dry. Suddenly, I saw his face turn down into a scowl as his eyes burned a hole in something just behind me.

Is he angry? What the hell does he have to be angry about?

I huffed just as I felt a hand at the small of my back, followed by Nathaniel's voice low in my ear. "I'm not Barack and I don't need you to be Michelle. But you *will* give *us* a chance."

* * *

Liam

I frowned as I stared across the room and saw the woman I'd been dreaming about and missing for five years as she was approached and touched by none other than Senator Nathaniel Roberts. His hand on her lower back was telling. It was an intimate touch. One Coral wouldn't allow without established permission. She didn't do public displays of affection.

I knew he'd had a thing for her since our Army days. I'd catch the long, lingering stares he'd give her. The extra flirty winks and smiles. Although I saw that Coral had taken a step back from the Senator's embrace, the image was already cemented in my brain, and it caused my blood to boil.

She shouldn't be over there with him. She should be with me.

I knew I should've been the last person to be jealous or possessive. After all, I was the one who'd snuck out on her like a thief in the night, leaving some lame ass note and nothing more. She deserved more than that. We'd been friends—best friends, for years. But I couldn't tell her the truth...that I left her to keep her safe. I'd stayed up many nights wondering if I'd made the right decision. As I looked over at Coral, who had now turned her full attention back to Nathaniel, I was leaning towards believing it was the wrong decision.

In that moment, I'd made a choice. I took a step towards where they were standing.

"Hey Liam, I think your father is looking for you."

That reminder by my head of security halted me in my tracks. My hand tightened into a fist as another source of ire flowed through me. It was a reminder of why I wasn't already across the room standing next to Coral. I had to remember to keep it together.

I nodded at Ron. "Alright, let's go find him." I pivoted to follow

Ron who had already spotted my father's location. That was a close call.

For the next few hours, I made nice and mingled with other guests, and took in the live performance of some pop star that had been hired to entertain for the night. I was able to catch up with some old army buddies of mine. Despite the distractions, at no point did I forget the tingling sensation in my belly that told me Coral was in the same room.

I could feel her energy even if I couldn't see her...and I did look. With every conversation I engaged in, I found my eyes scanning the room looking for her. Each time a glimpse of red caught my eye my heart rate sped up a little, but so far she had remained out of my line of sight. I was sure that was on purpose. No matter how much my brain told me that staying away from her was for the best, the part of me that had been missing without her wouldn't let me leave well enough alone.

A while later, I spotted her talking to a Congressman out of South Carolina. I couldn't be bothered to remember his name, but I knew his face. My feet began moving before my brain registered where they were going. As I made my way over, the Congressman made his departure, leaving her alone. I saw a waiter carrying champagne flutes approach her. With her back to me, I saw an opportunity.

"A glass of champagne, ma'am?" he asked, as soon as I reached her.

"She doesn't drink," I answered for her, causing her to turn and stare at me.

Those golden-hazel eyes flashed anger and she allowed her gaze to wander up and down my entire body. Despite the time and emotional distance between us, I wanted nothing more than to reach out and caress her cheek. I remembered the exact feel of that smooth skin under my fingertips. Luckily for me, I resisted. I saw a glimmer of emotion in her eyes—longing, sadness—before it was replaced with fire as her eyes came to rest on mine again.

"You changed your hair." The words fell from my lips as I took in the now short auburn curls.

She lifted a perfectly arched eyebrow. "Do I know you?"

She sent the dagger to my heart before turning and walking away. And I was thrust back into a memory of the first time I laid eyes on this woman. My best friend. My soulmate.

* * *

Fall 2000

"Welcome to Harvard's ROTC Program, recruits..." our PT instructor began his spiel that I was sure no one was listening to. It was our first week of early morning PT and my eyes were still fighting to remain open. A few of my friends behind me joked about some of the girls in our program. I'd admit I wasn't expecting there to be much eye candy in an ROTC program, but looking around I thought a few girls may be worth getting to know. I'd been fucking since the age of fifteen and college now offered a new world of random pussy to get lost in. I was up to the challenge.

"Damn, who's that?" I heard, Damon ask behind me, with awe in his voice.

I turned to see where he was looking and my breath caught. At about five-six, rich mocha skin, a heart shaped face, made less innocent by intense hazel eyes, there she stood. At eighteen, I still had yet to get used to my physical reactions towards the opposite sex, and I was surprised by my immediate physical response to her. She was dressed in the same ROTC sweat pants and shirt we all were in, but I could see those sweats hid a body made for sin. I heard Damon mumbling about wanting to get to know her and before he got the chance I cut him off and strolled over to her.

"Aww, man, you can't handle that."

I tossed him a middle finger and continued on. I was a cocky son of a bitch. I knew my height, tanned skin courtesy of many days spent underneath the Texas sun, and green eyes left women a decade older than me stuttering. I moved up close to her, and reached for a lock of her hair. Don't ask me why I did that, I just had an insane urge to touch her.

"Today might just be your lucky day," I murmured low in her ear, twirling her hair in between my fingers.

Stunned, she jumped back and glared at me. "Excuse you?"

Her voice sent shivers down my spine. Not taking heed of the fire blazing in her eyes, I took a step closer. "I said...today is your lucky day, sweetheart."

She paused and looked me up and down. "And why is that?" she asked.

I chuckled and gave her the most seductive wink I'd perfected. "Because you just caught my eye."

She looked me up and down again, scornfully, and in pure Coral fashion handed me my ass.

"If today is my lucky day, I should have stayed in bed. Don't ever touch me again." And then turned and walked away.

The snickers from behind me alerted me that Damon and our other friends heard the entire exchange. I tucked my proverbial tail between my legs and returned to my group, but continued to stare at the first girl to ever reject me and turn me on at the same time.

* * *

AFTER THAT INITIAL ENCOUNTER, my estimation of one Coral Coleman went up exponentially. With each PT and ROTC assignment she and I always seemed to come in as the top one and two. Sometimes she bested me. Other times I bested her. I never tried to hit on her after that and we managed to gain a mutual respect for one another. Our friendship didn't develop until a few months later; but once it did we were inseparable.

I came to know her as deeply as I allowed her to know me, which was also why I knew, my next move was one of my dumber moves. When she turned to walk away, I felt a piece of my soul leaving and I had to stop her. I grabbed her arm from behind. I immediately felt her stiffen and I braced myself.

"You of all people know better than to touch me like that," she gritted out through clenched teeth.

She was right. I did know better. Grabbing a woman from behind who experienced a childhood of abuse and had been to war was not the smartest idea. Especially not when this particular woman knew three different forms of martial arts. I'd seen her in hand-to-hand combat. Hell, she'd saved my ass as many times as I'd saved hers. I knew what she was capable of.

"Don't walk away." I released her arm and stepped back. I knew when to give Coral space.

"What?" she asked tersely.

I sighed, running my hand through my hair. There was so much I wanted to say and even more I wanted to do, but I wasn't free to do it for more reasons than one. I stared at her for a few moments, taking in the fact that we were in the same space after five years.

"How have you been?" I finally asked.

"Seriously?"

"Coral, I—"

"There you are," a familiar voice sounded from behind me.

I turned to see an unwelcome sight; a smiling Nathaniel Roberts, as he stared at Coral.

"I've been looking all over for you," he told her. Initially, he didn't acknowledge my presence, but shortly after he held out his hand. "Oh, Bennett. Long time no see. How have you been?" he asked with a look of warning in his eyes.

He was claiming what he believed was his territory.

He's got another think coming.

"Senator," I returned, gripping his hand a little tighter than necessary. "I've been well. A lot better now." I looked Coral straight in the eyes so she got my meaning.

"Well, I hope I wasn't interrupting anything," Roberts stated.

"Trust me, there's nothing you could do to interrupt me." I was tired of the bullshit. This dude had no idea the lengths I would go to for this woman.

"Is that right? Well—"

"You know, it's been great watching you two size-up who has the bigger dick, but I'm bored and I'm leaving. Have at it boys." Coral turned and walked away.

My instinct was to follow her, but just as I moved to do so, Nathaniel stepped in my path.

"I don't think so," he warned.

"Who the hell asked you to think, Roberts?" I stepped closer to him, and while I had a one-inch height advantage, he was not the least bit intimidated.

"She's moved on from whatever you two had between you," he said, turning to watch her as she moved further and further away from us.

I saw red when I watched his eyes land on the sway of her ass, encompassed perfectly in the fabric of that red dress. The leopard print heels were classic Coral. They showed her feminine, yet dangerous side.

"You think so?" I asked, my voice dangerously low.

He chuckled. "Oh yeah. By the way she was calling my name earlier this evening, I definitely think so."

I made a move to grab him by the lapels of his tux, but was stopped by Ron.

"Liam, we're in public."

I had no idea where he'd come from.

I didn't move back, but I took a breath to rein in my anger. "Just know, you're a temporary filler, Roberts. I've owned that woman since we were eighteen years old, and I will until the day I die. Don't ever forget that. And don't ever get in my face again about my woman. I don't care how long you've had this little crush on her, I will fuck you up over Coral," I growled.

I snatched away from Ron to walk away before I made good on my promise. I meant every word. I may have left Coral, but it was never meant to be a permanent situation. I'd always had every intention of claiming her as mine. That plan had never wavered.

CHAPTER 3

ou changed your hair.

Those words had been repeating over and over in my head the last month. It was the first time I had laid eyes on him in five years and that was the first thing he'd asked. As if we were old friends simply catching up. Maybe that's all it was to him. I didn't know if I was more angry or hurt. No explanation. No apology. Just some dumb observation about my hair. Yeah, it was longer and relaxed the last time I saw him and now it was short, curly, and a different color, but fuck that. He owed me more than a, "How have you been?"

Fuck. I hated that thinking about him tied me up in knots. That's not who I am.

I heard a male voice that I knew was my younger cousin, Jabari. "Yo, Coral! You in there?"

We were in the state-of-the-art gym we had built in our office building in the heart of Savannah. Jones & Associates Security was the name of the firm that I co-owned with my cousins, Quincy and Jabari. Quincy and I were more of the muscle, so to speak, while Jabari was the tech guy, although by looking at him you wouldn't assume, "tech geek."

"Let's spar," I said, tossing a pair of boxing gloves at Jabari. Boxing was my first learned form of fighting, and my first love. I learned at the community center in my neighborhood in the Bronx. The coaches were hesitant to show a twelve-year-old girl the technique of boxing, but I wanted something that would help me feel less vulnerable at home and on the streets.

When the one parent you were left with opted to take all his anger out on you, you found ways to cope. And since I had my little sister to watch out for, I let him take it out on me to keep her safe. Boxing allowed me to feel safer the older and stronger I got.

"A'ight. Five rounds, though. I'm not going twenty rounds with you again. Plus, we've got some business in the office to address."

I grinned. I had been putting Jabari through the ringer over the last month with our sparring sessions. But at six-two and solid muscle, he could take it.

"Don't be a baby this time, okay?" I taunted.

"Whatever, just strap up."

We spent the next hour going toe-to-toe. Jabari pulled no punches…just the way I liked it. He knew the truth was that I sometimes held back with him. I could handle myself, and the extra tension I'd been feeling lately from thinking more and more about Li had me on edge. That and I'd yet to find any more intel on Ghost. I was becoming more aggravated by the day. It was either hit the gym for sparring or I was going to lose it, and that would not be good for anyone in my vicinity.

After our sparring session, I headed to the shower to get ready for the workday. Quincy was out of town on business for the next few weeks. I hadn't told anyone about seeing Liam in DC, and I knew out of everyone, Quincy would be the angriest about it. He was the only one who knew about what happened right after Liam left without any explanation and married someone else. He'd had a special hatred for Li ever since. I was also sure that Quincy was deflecting some anger toward Liam, but that was a story for another day.

I finished showering in the private bathroom and slid on a pair of dark blue skinny jeans, an off-the-shoulder cream sweater, and a pair of black ankle boots. Perfect outfit for the late fall weather. It was time to get my day started.

* * *

"Coral," our office administrative assistant, Elsie, called out. "Don't forget your eleven o'clock with Jabari in his office. You're meeting a new potential client," she advised.

"Thanks, Els. I'll be there."

I turned back to the papers on my desk. I was going over a few old cases and making sure the paperwork was in order for all of the files. I had a conference call with another long-term client at nine-thirty to discuss their security detail over the holiday season. I spent the morning lost in the pile of work on my desk and making phone calls. I was planning to be out of town for the next few weeks, and then heading back to Colombia to do some more digging to find Ghost. By the time I realized it, it was time for me to head down the hall to my meeting with Jabari and our potential client.

I grabbed my mug and headed down the hall to make a fresh cup of green tea. Mug and tablet in hand, I made my way to Jabari's office. Before I entered, I heard two deep voices. One was Jabari's and the other I hadn't heard in years, but remembered without hesitation. My pulse quickened at the thought of who else I might find as I entered the office. I inhaled deeply and rounded the office, knocking on the opened door to alert the men of my presence. I was met with Jabari's dark brown eyes and another pair of green eyes. *If it's not one Bennett, it's another.*

Jeremy stood to greet me. "Well, aren't you a sight for sore eyes."

"Jeremy, to what do I owe the pleasure?" I asked as we hugged each other. I was in awe seeing Jeremy so soon after seeing Liam. Although they were first cousins, they could easily pass for fraternal twins. They shared green eyes, height and build, but Liam was blond, where Jeremy was dark-haired and had a slightly darker hue than Li.

25

"Oh, you know me, darling.' Just in the neighborhood," he intoned in that familiar Texas twang, the ever-present toothpick between his lips.

"Cut the shit, Jer. What are you really doing here?"

At that, he tipped his head back and let a low chuckle emanate from his core. Admittedly, I'd missed that sound. I hadn't seen Jeremy in nearly six years.

"I see you haven't changed, Scorpion."

I narrowed my eyes at him. I didn't like being called by my codename in the office or around family. That name represented a side of me I reserved for out in the field.

Jeremy held up his hands. "I know. I know. It's Coral 'round these parts. Anyway, I was just talking to Jabari here about some work I needed done and your company was the best fit for it."

I looked over at Jabari who hadn't said a word since I entered his office. He looked at me and raised his eyebrows. I looked back at Jeremy.

"What's the job?"

"I need you to find a leak in the company."

I knew the answer to my next question, but I asked it anyway. "What company?"

"Bennett Industries."

"There's a second Bennett Industries?"

For a split second, a look of confusion crossed Jeremy's face before he got my meaning.

He shook his head. "No darlin'. It's the same one."

"So, there's a new CEO?" I asked.

"Nope again. You *know* who the CEO is."

"In that case, I don't think so," I said, turning to leave.

"Coral, wait." It was the first time Jabari had spoken up. "Hear the man out at least," he insisted.

I looked at Jabari and then back to Jeremy. My curiosity was peaked. I walked over to the chair in front of Jabari's desk and sat. "Talk," I instructed him.

"When Liam became CEO of Bennett Industries, one of the first things he did was to thoroughly go over the company's financials. He noticed some inconsistencies, year after year. As a result, he hired a guy named Larry, who was a forensic accountant, about three years ago. No one knew that Larry's *actual* role was to investigate the company's financial history. To everyone except me and Liam, he was just one of the regular accounting managers. Anyway, about a month ago, we got a call from Larry saying he'd finally put two and two together, and that we needed to meet with him so that he could tell us who was behind all this.

He insisted it be in person. Since both Liam and I were out of town on business, we set the meeting for a few days later. Well, Larry never made it because two days later he died in a car accident." Jeremy paused and looked me right in the eyes, "The police ruled his death an accident, but that was too much of a coincidence...and I don't believe in coincidences."

Neither do I, I thought silently. I'd seen too much to believe in coincidences.

"This wasn't some random accountant who stumbled upon some information. He was hired to look into Bennett Industries' past. We weren't able to get much from him in our short phone call, but he mentioned something about a Ghost."

I sat up in my seat for the first time since sitting down.

Jeremy noticed my change in demeanor. "That ring a bell?" he asked.

"You've got my full attention now," I said.

"There's a file he had that we have yet to find. I think the information he found is in that file. Coral, I came to you because I've researched your company. I know you guys can handle this and I knew my cousin wouldn't have asked. I think he might be in danger."

The thought of Liam in danger was like a punch to the gut. I had already made my decision to take the job at the mention of "Ghost." But hearing that the same person who was targeting me may be targeting Liam made me even surer of this. Maybe I could kill two birds with one stone, get this Ghost off my back and keep Li out of harm's way. I didn't stop to think about why I cared so much about Liam's safety; it just felt like second nature. I told myself I was just returning the favor to an old friend.

CHAPTER 4

"**Y**ou did what?" I asked, eerily calm as I peered down at my cousin over the massive Cherrywood desk in my office. I had just learned that my cousin, who was like a brother to me, had gone behind my back and done the one thing he knew would piss me off to no end. As I stood there contemplating leaping over my desk to snatch him out of his seat, he had the nerve to look me with an air of nonchalance.

"Be careful, cousin. It's been a few years since you've been in battle. I wouldn't do what your eyes are telling me you're considering doing," Jeremy warned. But if he thought he intimidated me, he'd better think again.

"I will kick your ass for this. Why the hell would you do this?" I folded my arms over my chest to keep them from wrapping around Jeremy's damn neck. I was confused as to why Jeremy would go all the way to Savannah to hire Coral and her family to help our company out of this situation.

"Because Jones & Associates Security is one of the best at what they do." He shrugged.

Coral's company specialized in high-end security contracts, private investigations, and a whole host of "special favors" that were often needed by powerful business and political leaders. I'd been doing my own research on her company. On the one hand, I knew that they, particularly Coral, could help find whoever was behind threatening my company. On the other hand, I feared that Coral would be too good at her job, putting her right in the center of danger. I'd spent the past five years away from her trying to keep her out of danger. Of course, that had backfired. Not only had I spent five years without the woman I loved, but she ended up taking on a career that was extremely dangerous. From my own research, I found out that she'd opened the firm with her cousins only in the last year and a half, which still left three years I'd spent searching for her after I left. I had my suspicions on what she'd spent those years doing, and I wanted to kick myself for ever letting her out of my sight.

"You and I both know Coral is the right person to handle this job. We need answers and from the research I've done, Jones & Associates will help us get those answers. We need to get to the bottom of whoever killed Larry," Jeremy implored.

I knew he was right about getting to whoever was behind our company's problematic financials. The person who in all likelihood was responsible for Larry's death. I took that personally. Since becoming the head of Bennett Industries five years ago, I prided myself on expanding not only the oil, gas operations, and the expansion into the hospitality world, but to also treat my employees very well—the opposite of how my father treated anyone he deemed below him.

Jeremy was the head of our hospitality division, running our ten hotels located throughout Texas, Louisiana, Arizona and Southern California. I'd made it my mission to bring Bennett Industries into the twenty-first century by focusing on renewable energy sources, and expanding our portfolio so that oil wasn't our only source of revenue. So far, I'd done a good job and that meant the first step of my original plan was working out well.

"There are thousands of security firms in this damn country. You just had to pick the one that I wouldn't want working this case. What the fuck are you trying to do?"

I tried hard to restrain my anger, but I knew I was close to shouting. The longer he sat there with that smug look on his face, the more I contemplated how long it would take me to beat his ass before my assistant became alarmed by the noise and called security.

"You know as well as I do that they are the most qualified." Jeremy leveled his green eyes at me and frowned. "You've been on this shit long enough. It's time you do what you set out to do more than five years ago and go get your woman."

As if it were that simple.

"You have no idea—"

"Oh, I have an idea alright. I remember exactly why you told me you left her all those years ago, and I've seen every day for the last five years how it eats away at you. I see the days you spend working well into the night just to avoid thinking about her. If it wasn't for Laura—"

"Don't bring her into this," I warned.

Jeremy dismissively waved his hand, and continued with his statement. "If it wasn't for Laura, you'd never leave this damn office, working yourself into an early grave. All so you can avoid feeling lost because the one person you know is your soulmate isn't with you."

I stood there shocked. Jeremy consistently teased me throughout my friendship with Coral about me wanting more. I always dismissed his allegations, not wanting to reveal the feelings I'd had since the first time I laid eyes on her. When I had to leave her, he was the one person I told why, and he supported my plan to get rid of the problem. Now, he was telling me to throw out the original plan and go after Coral.

I scoffed. "Are you crazy? You know exactly why I left her and why I don't want her involved in this. So fucking what, I spend a few nights a week in my damn office. You aren't complaining about all the work I put in when your ass is out partying with the high rollers."

I knew that was a low blow. Jeremy had a party boy reputation, but he'd been trying to let go of that image so that people could see him as a serious and competent business professional. Right then, I didn't care about hurting his feelings. I was pissed at him for going behind my back.

"Fuck you, Liam."

"No, *fuck you*! You knew I wouldn't want this. I don't give a shit what you do, but you better call Jones & Associates and tell them we don't need their services!"

"I can't do that."

"Why the fuck not?"

"Because," he paused looking at his Patek Philippe watch. "She should be here any minute."

His smirk told me he was enjoying seeing me seethe.

"So you waited until the last minute to tell me because you knew there was nothing I could do about it. I'm going to kick your ass."

The chuckle he let out pissed me off even more.

"You think I'm kidding? Call them and tell them we are no longer in need of their services."

"I'm not doing that."

"Yes, the fuck you are. I don't want her here!" I slammed my hand on my desk. The thought of Coral getting mixed up my company's mess had all my protective instincts coming out. I was seeing red.

Suddenly, a feminine voice with a hint of edge in it sounded from my office doorway. "Calm down, Liam. It's not like I was jumping up and down to take this case myself."

I had long memorized every intonation of that voice. I spent many nights dreaming about, and hell, jerking off to, memories of that voice. Especially when it moaned when I was deep in—

"Well, Ms. Coleman, how nice of you to finally join us," Jeremy greeted Coral, interrupting my thoughts.

I finally glanced toward my office doorway and took her in. There she stood at five-feet eight inches, had smooth brown skin that reminded me of my favorite Godiva chocolates, and piercing hazel eyes that saw everything. She was dressed in a pair of dark blue skinny jeans, a black t-shirt, white blazer that was rolled up at the sleeves, and black pumps. It was a simple ensemble, but she filled it out to perfection. I took in her hair, marveling at how different it looked from the way she wore it years ago. But this short look worked for her. The auburn colored coily curls on top gave her a bit of edge that I knew fit her personality, while the cut itself allowed for her naturally high cheekbones and eye color to stand out. She was beautiful.

She leveled one of her no-nonsense looks at me. "If you're done gawking, we can get started on this case."

"I wasn't gawking," I lied, lamely.

Her full lips turned down into a frown indicating she knew I was lying.

"Here darlin', why don't you come in and we can discuss the specifics of this case. It's been a few months since we last met and I'm sure you may need to go over some details," Jeremy instructed.

Coral strutted into my office, and instead of sitting in the chair directly in front of my desk, she glanced around and went over to the cream, leather loveseat that sat against the wall across from my desk.

I raised an eyebrow at her choice but remained quiet.

"So gentlemen, let's get started, shall we? The sooner we can get this wrapped up, the sooner I can be out of your hair and on my way." She smiled, but it didn't reach her eyes as she stared right at me.

I swallowed the lump in my throat. I knew I had hurt her feelings. She'd never say as much, but walking in and hearing me say how much I didn't want her there had to be difficult. I couldn't tell her that the truth was I wanted nothing more than for her to be by my side every minute of every day.

* * *

CORAL

My heart sank when I walked up to Liam's door and heard him yelling at Jeremy that he didn't want me there. I quickly let that emotion switch to anger because I was done being hurt over Liam. I felt safer with my anger. I was pissed because first of all, I'd never done anything to him to make him want to keep his distance. Even after he declared to be in love with me only to run off with the beauty queen and get married, I never gave him any trouble. I didn't even bother to ask him why. And second of all, this was someone who was once my best friend. We'd spent a decade being the most important people in one another's lives. He knew me inside and out and I thought I knew him. And I was not someone who got close to others. So yeah, hearing him say he wanted nothing to do with me pissed me off. But I wouldn't let his funky attitude deter me. I was there to save his company, and to save my own hide.

In the last few months since Jeremy came to Savannah, I'd been tying up loose ends with our other clients to make sure I could give this case my complete attention. Whoever this Ghost was already killed two of my former colleagues, and he might've also been after Liam. And like they say, 'The enemy of my enemy is my friend'. So like it or not, Liam and I had a common enemy, making us friends, at least until we got to whoever this was. Once business with him was over, I could go on about my merry way, and he could continue to live in married bliss.

Even as I thought my plan through, I felt the twinge of pain in my chest at the thought of never seeing Liam again. The knowledge that he was married to someone else still stung as it did five years ago, but I'm good at faking it when necessary. So I did what I do best. I ignored my emotional turmoil and got down to business.

"Okay, since I'm here, let's say you make this trip worth my while, and start from the beginning." I spoke to both men, but never took my eyes off Liam.

CHAPTER 5

*L*iam

Her scent was killing me. It had to be some mixture of coconut oil, cocoa butter and her natural scent. I remembered that smell very well and as we walked along my offices, introducing her to my staff, my fingers itched to reach out and touch. We'd spent the better part of an hour going over the details of the problems we were having. Jeremy did most of the talking, and every once in awhile Coral would glance up at me and glare. I knew she was pissed from what she'd heard when she first entered my office. I felt like a heel and wanted to kick myself.

Once Jeremy left, Coral asked to be introduced to all my department heads and to see Larry's office. Plans for later included taking her on a tour of the oil and energy facilities, that were a part from headquarters. As we walked into Larry's office an eerie feeling came over me, seeing his empty chair. Larry and I weren't close, but he was a good employee. To think his working for me was what got him killed infuriated me.

"And he kept all his files on his work computer or did he ever work from home?" Coral asked.

I looked up to see her staring at me, and for a split second I saw a look of what I thought was empathy before her eyes shuttered and she was all business again.

"What did you ask me?"

"I asked if all his work files were kept on his office desktop or if he ever worked from home?"

I sighed. "All of our department heads have a company issued laptop they can use from either work or home. Larry worked from home one to two days a week. He said it helped to minimize distractions. Most of the department heads work from home some of the time."

"I don't see any laptop here," she said, gently pulling open the desk drawers and peeking in.

I cocked my head to the side. "We've been looking for it. I personally made a trip to the home he shared with his fiancé to ask if he'd left it at home. It wasn't recovered from his vehicle either. We're still looking," I stated.

"Have you looked through his personal accounts to see if he owned a safe deposit box? Maybe he hid it there."

I nodded agreeing with her. "I have my head of security looking into it and maybe speak with Larry's fiancé again." I sighed dreading having to bother Lisa, Larry's fiancé who was still grieving.

Coral stood in front of me, and rested her hand on my forearm comfortingly. "I can do that if it's too much for you," she commented.

Even through my suit jacket I felt her warmth and it felt like it was thawing a piece of my heart that had been frozen over. Unconsciously, I moved to put my hand over hers to keep her there. We stood that way, for what seemed like forever, and yet not long enough. Suddenly, Coral pulled away and took a step back, clearing her throat.

Quickly recovering, I told her, "That won't be necessary. I know Lisa, so the question might be better coming from me."

Coral simply nodded and stepped around me, exiting the office. "I want to meet your head of security before we head out to your other locations," she said over her shoulder.

This is not going to go over well, I thought as I pulled out my phone to text my head of security to come to my office.

* * *

*C*ORAL

"How long have you worked with your head of security?" I asked, sitting back on the loveseat in Liam's office. I was relieved when he opted to sit behind his desk. I aimed to keep my distance as much as possible. I didn't know what that little stare down in Larry's office was, but I was not about to let it happen again.

"For a few years now, bu-"

Knock! Knock! "Hey Liam, you wanted to se--"

I paused and turned as I heard the familiar, yet unwanted voice. I took in Ron's muscular frame. He was not especially tall, only a few inches taller than me at five-ten, dark brown hair and eyes, golden colored skin. He would be attractive by most conventional standards. As we took each other in, I noticed the right side of his mouth kick up into a sneer. In less than a split second the look was gone and he plastered a phony smile on his face.

"Coral Coleman. How nice to see you again. To what do we owe the pleasure?" he greeted me, but moved towards Liam's desk to stand at its side.

"Good to see you too, Ron. I'm here working to find out what happened to Larry in accounting."

Ron's eyebrows quirked up in obvious surprise at my little revelation, before he recovered and looks towards Liam. "I thought that was just an accident."

Now this I found a little intriguing. Liam hadn't told his head of security that he suspected Larry's death wasn't an accident. *Interesting.* Ron was a part of our unit during the second Iraq tour. He was a few years younger than us, but he took to Liam. Li, took him under his wing and showed him the ropes. Personally, I never liked him. He had a way of making me felt as if I was intruding anytime he and Liam were together and I came around. Truth is, Liam barely tolerated him at first, but after serving together they developed a friendship. From where I sat, it looked like that friendship had outlasted the one Liam and I had. Who would have thought?

"There are some underlying circumstances that lead us to believe it was more than just an accident," Liam answered. "Coral's here to help us get to the bottom of it."

I noticed Liam's eyes bulge slightly, eyebrows raised and mouth parted in what looked like a micro expression of fear. Of course, in less than a tenth of a second it was gone. I can read most people like a book, but the one area where my special talent failed me was reading those closest to me. It had always been difficult to read Liam because feelings and emotions got in the way. But I couldn't ignore what I saw. I believed it was fear and that was revealing. The Liam I knew wasn't afraid of shit. We've kicked down doors together in Iraq and Afghanistan, dodged bullets, and stood tall as we took on enemy combatants. Rarely did I ever see fear. Except that one time…

"Alright, what is it you need us to do?" Ron asked.

I turned my attention to him, ridding myself of past memories, and began telling him what we were going to do to get to find out who may be out to get Bennett Industries. I instructed Ron to gather files for all department heads and to set up a place where we could conduct one-on-one recorded interviews with the employees.

"You're going to interview all our employees?" he asked.

"No," I shook my head. "You are."

"What?"

I looked to Liam who I saw was following my strategy. This was old hat for us. We often interrogated suspected Al Qaeda members and insurgents together overseas.

"You're going to interview the employees while I watch. We'll film the interviews and analyze them to see if anyone appears suspicious."

Ron scoffed. "How are we going to do that? If anyone is involved in this, they're not just going to announce themselves after a few questions."

I smirked at Ron. "I have my ways."

"Liam, I don-"

Liam held up his hand, cutting Ron off. "She knows what she's doing," he said with total confidence staring at me.

For some reason hearing him defend me sent a chill down my

spine, and I bit the inside of my cheek to keep from smiling. I didn't like the reactions this man could elicit from me with just a few words or a simple glance.

Once Ron left to set up his task, Liam and I headed out to go see his other plants on the outskirts of Dallas. We visited a few of the oil drilling sites and talk with a few of the employees there. After the oil sites, Liam had his driver take us to another of the facilities.

"This is where we do R&D for alternative energies."

I turned to look at him as the town car pulls up to the huge industrial looking building.

"Tell me about it," I said as he held the door open for me and we enter the building.

Liam's smile lit up and those damned butterflies started fluttering in the pit of my stomach.

"One hundred percent of this facility's power is via solar power."

I nodded attentively, remembering the solar panels that were on the roof as we pulled up.

"But solar energy isn't the only alternative energy method we're looking into. In this facility we have researchers working on solar and biomass energies. Right now, our headquarters downtown is twenty percent run by alternative energies. Our goal is to increase that to fifty percent over the next five years," he stated proudly as he continued to show me around the facility. All around there were employees in lab coats using microscopes, filling beakers and otherwise occupied as they bustled about.

I smiled without realizing it, proud to see one of Liam's dreams coming true right before me. While in undergrad and in the Army we stayed up many a nights as he told me his dreams of reducing his family's business' dependence on oil. While the black gold had brought his family multi-generational wealth, he was heavily concerned about the environmental impact of drilling, oil leaks, and even the threat of oil explosion or spills. "You're doing it. You're accomplishing what you set out to do," I said, admiring the sight before me.

He turned and stared at me with a half-smile. That smile told me he was proud of what he was accomplishing, but there was something in his eyes. "Almost everything I set out to do."

His gaze lingered on me for another second before he turned to show me something else. I didn't dwell on the moment. I didn't want to talk myself into seeing something that may not have actually been there. I tamped down on the longing rising in my gut and followed as he showed me the rest of the plant.

We remained at the plant for a little while longer, before heading back to his headquarters. Though there was still a couple of hours left in his work day, I prepared to head out early to go back to my hotel and organize my thoughts and notes for the next steps. "Thank you for showing me around," I said as I packed up my things.

"No problem," he returned as he pulled on his suit jacket.

"I-" I paused as my eye catches Liam's hand twisting the cufflink on his sleeve. I recognized it immediately. He must have noticed my hesitation because he looked up at me. His hand stilled as he registered my shock at seeing the cufflink. They were made of sterling silver and had his initials "LB" engraved into them. I knew them because they cost me a pretty penny to purchase and have them embroidered for our college graduation. I didn't know why seeing him in the gift I purchased for him all those years ago struck me so hard, but it did.

"You kept them," I stated just above a whisper. Being that he was shocked that I was even coming today, I doubted he wore them just for me.

"Yeah," he smiled lightly.

"I bet your wife isn't too happy about you wearing a gift from another woman." I didn't even know where those words came from as they slipped out of my mouth. But I'd said it, the elephant in the room. Liam's wife. The woman he left me for. I avoided eye contact as I placed my cell phone in my bag and prepared to leave.

"I don't have a wife."

That stopped me in my tracks and I looked up to find his eyes on me. I noted the sincerity in them. Liam was no longer married. For some reason this made me even angrier. He promised me forever only to up and leave for a woman he didn't make it to six years with. Without a word, I stood and headed towards the door.

"I'll be back nine am sharp tomorrow," I said, reaching for the doorknob.

He'd gotten up from his desk and was halfway across the room as he said, "I searched for you."

I paused to turn to him, needing to hear what he had to say.

"Right after I left I came back to look for you. You were gone. For years I searched for you," he admitted.

I lowered my gaze not wanting to meet his. I felt the sincerity in his words, but I was confused as to why he would search for me. He left me. Not the other way around.

"I searched using some pretty powerful contacts. They came up with nothing." His voice held a hint of accusation. "There's only a few organizations I know that can so thoroughly erase a person's trace like that. And all of them are known by their three letter abbreviations."

I turned my head to the side, continuing to avoid his gaze and bite my inner cheek.

He was asking me a question. He wanted to know where I'd been for years, but he also knew I couldn't answer. I turned and stared at a spot over his shoulder neither confirming nor denying his suspicions. My silence was answer enough for him.

"It wouldn't be the NSA because I had a connect there and they couldn't find you. The FBI would have been easier to find you in..." he trailed off looking down at me. "The Agency, huh? You went and worked for them?" There was anger in his voice.

"Li..." I made my eyes meet his using the nickname that only I was allowed to call him.

The Agency, otherwise known as the CIA, was indeed who I spent working for the first three years after Liam left.

"I thought you didn't want to be anyone's spy," he stated reminding me of a conversation we had about our plans after the Army.

I told him that while my skillset may be appealing to the CIA I didn't want to spend my life being anyone's spy and living a double life overseas.

"Plans change," I retorted, now looking him directly in the eye. By this time he was so close to me that air could barely pass between our bodies.

"So they do," he said a second before grabbing my face and pressing his lips to mine before I could react.

My first instinct was to pull away, but his lips on mine felt too good. Before I knew it a small moan escaped my mouth and caused my lips to part. Liam's insistent tongue wasted no time snaking its way into my mouth. He let his tongue explore my mouth before pulling back and licking my lips. He bit my lower lip and then used his tongue to soothe the bite before spearing my mouth with his tongue again. This wasn't a sweet, patient kiss. It was full of heat, need and dare I say possession? The kiss ended much too soon for my liking when Liam pulled back. Still holding my face between his hands he asked "Are you still with Nate?"

That question was like cold water to my veins. I blinked shocked, and then angry that he had the balls to ask me about Nathaniel while he had a whole wife--at least he used to.

"What the hell kind of question is that?" I demanded pulling out of his hold.

"A legitimate one. Answer it."

"No."

"Why not?"

"Because it's none of your damn business. For the rest of my time here I expect you to keep your lips to yourself."

He scoffed. "Don't count on it, CeCe."

He turned the tables, now referring to me as the nickname only he ever called me. It sent my already erratic nerves into a frenzy. I needed to get out of here.

"You better if you want to keep them," I threatened before turning throwing the door open to leave. I moved so fast I nearly knocked Ron over who was coming to enter the office, but I didn't miss the chuckle from Liam behind my back as I stormed out.

* * *

Liam

"So Coral's back?" Ron asked, as I continued to stare at Coral's backside as she walked away.

That woman's got a great pair of legs and a plump, taught ass to boot.

"Yes, she is," I smiled.

"That's good if it helps us find out if there is anything to Larry's death."

I felt Ron's pause and I knew I wasn't going to like what he had to say next.

"Does she know about Laura?" he asked.

That question was the one to wipe the smile from my face completely. My heart skipped a beat.

"No," I responded, turning to go sit behind my desk. "Tell me how we're going to do these interviews," I demanded, switching topics. I didn't want to think of the question he'd just asked me.

CHAPTER 6

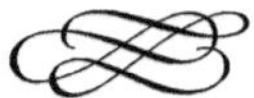

oral

I stretched out on the plush bed in my huge guest suite. I hadn't planned to stay in a suite, but when I checked in I saw my room had been upgraded. I knew it was Jeremy's doing. As I stared out the floor to ceiling windows towards the Dallas skyline I sighed heavily. Some days it felt like I lived in hotels. Even though I owned a condo in Savannah, I was barely there enough for it to feel like home. I knew my family wished I were around more, and truthfully, I did too. I wanted to get this case wrapped up and find out whoever this Ghost was and eliminate him before he killed me. That was the only way I could spend more time with my family without endangering them.

Pulling out my cell phone I saw it was only around seven. I opted to call Stacey, my younger sister to see how she was doing. Stacey lived in Atlanta and recently married, Andre Collins, a wealthy businessman in the city. I actually knew his older brother, Nikola from the Army.

"Hey, sis," Stacey's breathless voice greeted me.

"Hey, you. You sound like you were rushing. I didn't interrupt anything did I?"

"No, I actually just got home from running some errands after work. I'm surprised you're calling during the week though and in the evening."

I chuckled at her statement. It was a running joke between the two of us that I usually called her early Saturday mornings. She used to grumble about me calling so early on the weekend, especially since she used to dance ballet and had late night performances on Fridays. But, I started calling whenever I was free and it just became a habit that Saturday mornings were reserved to catch up with my sister, no matter where in the world I was. She dealt with it.

"Yeah well, I was free and was missing you so I thought I'd give you a call. How are you?"

"Oh," she paused, "I miss you too. Nothing much is going on over here between work and-"

"Being a newlywed," I laughed. I knew her new husband kept her busy. The man had a bit of a possessive streak when it came to my sister, but he also had a heart of gold and loved Stacey unconditionally. I could tell he was good for her.

"Yeah that too. Andre and I are going to Seattle in a couple of weeks. He has some business to take care of out there, and I decided to take a few days off to go visit my old home base. We're going to take in a performance at my old dance company."

I smiled. Stacey had loved ballet since she took her first class at five years old. She had fulfilled her dreams of dancing professionally, dancing at the Pacific Northwest Ballet in Seattle, until the age of twenty-five when an injury sidelined her. She went through a lot with that loss, but eventually regrouped and went back to school to become a social worker. It took her years to be able to watch ballet again, though. I knew Andre had something to do with that. And for that, I was grateful to him. I never told Stacey, but on her deathbed my mother made me promise to watch out for her. It was a promise I'd done my best to keep since I was nine years old.

"I'm so happy for you, Stace. I know that trip is well-earned."

"Thanks, sis. Enough about me. What are you up to these days? What far off country or continent are you in now?"

"I'm actually not that far. I'm in the great state of Texas working a case." I shut my mouth before offering too many details. I didn't want her to know I was in Dallas because I ran the risk of her possibly guessing that I was working with Liam. She didn't know everything that went on in our relationship, but she did know how close we were, and then suddenly we weren't. I think she suspects more happened between us than just a friendship. My sister being as smart as she was, and always wanting to be there for me the way I'd been there for her likely wouldn't let it drop. I already had enough on my mind.

"I know you won't give me the details, but are you at least being safe?" She tried to make the question sound lighthearted, but I heard the underlying worry in her voice. I was used to it by now. I'd called my sister from war zones and other dangerous locales. She had a right to be worried, but it still made my chest ache a little to know she was so fearful of my work.

"I'm being as safe as I know how to be." That was my honest answer. Truth was, I couldn't eliminate all threats and I didn't want to lie to her and tell her I wasn't in any danger. That's just not the way my life was.

"Good. I trust you to be smart," she stated.

We spent the next twenty minutes catching up. She told me about her social work in an eating disorder facility and how much she was enjoying it. I could hear the passion in her voice. I felt proud remembering the tears she cried in my arms coming to the realization that her dreams of becoming a prima ballerina would never come true. The happiness in her voice lifted a weight off my shoulder I hadn't even known was there. I breathed a little easier hearing my sister talk about new treatment options and expanding her facility's reach to working-class and women of color. Before hanging up she made me promise to still call her at my usual Saturday time. Next, I dialed another number.

"It's about time you called. I was beginning to think you'd forgotten all about me." The airy voice tried to sound admonishing, but also held a hint of laughter.

I chuckled. "Whatever, Tasha. We spoke three days ago."

She faked a pout. "Three days is too long."

I shook my head. Tasha was what I would consider the closest thing I had to a friend these days. I told her more about my life than I told my family. Mine and Tasha's actual connection was a complicated one, and she didn't like to discuss her past, so we rarely talked about how we actually knew each other. Those were painful memories for her.

"Anyway, where are you now?"

Before I caught the words they slipped out, "I'm in Dallas." I guessed I was feeling the need to share with someone what was happening in my life.

"Dallas? Hmm-wait, isn't that where *he who shall not be named* lives?"

I sighed. She too knew of my complicated relationship with Liam. "Yes."

"And?"

"And what?" I snapped.

"Don't play dumb with me, Coral. And are you working with Liam?"

I pushed out a heavy breath as my only response.

"Oh my God, you are. Is this the first time you've seen him in how many years?"

"More than five. Well, except last October when I went to DC."

"You've been holding out. Tell me," she demanded.

Usually, I could keep my business private, but I wanted to share with someone what I'd been feeling the last few months. First seeing Liam at the ball, and now working on this case in such close proximity. I told Tasha mostly everything, keeping a few details to myself.

"Well, what are you going to do?"

"Nothing. I'm going to work this case and then move on like always."

"Coral," she hesitated, "I think you need to talk to Liam. Maybe he didn't leave for the reasons you think he did. Maybe..." she trailed off.

"Maybe what? You know something I don't?" I asked. Tasha knew

Liam. They'd met years earlier when Tasha had come back into my life after years apart.

"No. I just remember the way he used to look at you. I know what love looks like and it was written all over his face."

I ran my hand over my short curls and stared out the window to the darkening sky. "I don't want to talk about it, Tash. Tell me how the new book is coming," I deflected. For the past five years Tasha had worked full-time as a sci-fi writer. Her books were extremely popular and they centered on a young African-American girl in alternate universes saving the planet Earth from destruction. I loved her stories and I could tell that Tash was writing for the girl she was who needed saving. She'd made the New York Times' bestseller list multiple times. Despite her success the most fascinating part was no one had any idea who she was. She wrote under a pen name and did not do public interviews. I knew why she refused to go public and given her history and I could understand why.

"Nice deflection, but I'll let it slide because I need to bounce a couple ideas off you anyway," she responded.

We spent another thirty minutes talking about some ideas Tasha had come up with for future books. She then told me where she was stuck in the current book she was writing. The heroine was in a pretty precarious situation and Tasha had no idea how to get her out of it. I did more listening than talking. I knew Tasha didn't need my input. She was a phenomenal writer who just sometimes needed to hear things out loud to work through them. Sure enough, by the end of our conversation, Tasha worked out how to get her heroine out of her sticky situation and on to saving the world. As we hang up, I smiled knowing two of the most important women in my life were doing well. Given where we all came from, we shouldn't have made it this far, but we did. I wasn't one for religion, but as I stared out my hotel window I closed my eyes thanking God and asked Him to continue keeping my family safe.

CHAPTER 7

*L*iam

"And you've rescheduled my afternoon meeting for next week, right?" I asked my assistant, Darlene. I came into the office early to get a phone meeting and some paperwork out of the way. I wanted this day cleared out. There was a part of my business that I did not show Coral yesterday that I was looking forward to showing her later on in the day. I knew she was going to spend the first part of the day going over camera footage with Ron and our security team. After that, I wanted to show her a little surprise.

"Yes, sir," Darlene answered. "Your three o'clock has been rescheduled for the same time next Tuesday and I've ordered your lunch to be delivered at 1pm."

I nodded in approval. "Thank you, Darlene. Just make sure the car is ready to pick us up at two."

Darlene nodded in agreement and left me to my work. I began filling out some forms that needed to be completed and scanning some documents to make sure I had them on file. Before I knew it, I heard a knock on my door.

"Good morning," Coral uttered in a voice that although was not meant to be seductive, still caused goosebumps to rise on my skin.

I pivoted around in my chair and gave her a smile. Just twenty-four hours ago I was in this very same spot demanding Jeremy tell her we no longer needed her services. Now, I contemplated sending Jere a damn thank you letter. I couldn't believe how having her this close had brightened my mood.

I stood from my chair. "Good morning, Coral," I greeted, as I unbuttoned my Armani suit jacket. Although she tried not to, I saw her eyes trail up and down my body; her gaze softening as she realized I was once again wearing the cufflinks she gifted me. Unbeknownst to her, I wore these cufflinks to work at least three times a week. It was my way of keeping her close.

"I had my assistant go out and get some green tea from Starbucks. Seems we ran out in the office kitchen," I said holding up the grande cup of hot tea.

She half smiled up at me as she took the cup from my hand. "You didn't have to do that. Thank you." Her fingers grazed mine and the pulse of awareness that shot through both of us had us staring in each other's eyes; causing her to be the first to take a step back.

As I watched her take a sip of her tea I nearly groaned at the sight of her full, gloss coated lips wrapped around the edge of the cup. I imagined her lips wrapped around something else...

"I'm heading to Ron's office to organize and to analyze some of the interview video footage," she stated, her words break into my train of thought.

"Right. Ron told me about that. I also arranged for us to see another part of my business this afternoon after lunch."

Her eyebrows rose as she gave me a questioning look. "I thought we saw everything, except the hotel side of your business yesterday. I doubt this has anything to do with the hotels and spas segment of the company."

"I agree. Jeremy has his own separate accounting team and employees. Our companies are housed under Bennett Industries, but run as separate companies. Whatever this danger is, it likely has to do with the energy and oil sector of the business. But that's not where I was taking you. It's our community relations and outreach sector I wanted to share with you. I'll tell you more later. I've scheduled lunch at one pm, here in my office and right afterwards, we'll leave," I explained, once again sitting down behind my desk.

Coral tossed me a confused, yet resigned look. "Okay, I'm heading down to Ron's office now. I'll be up in a few hours."

Those few hours seemed like they dragged on forever. I found myself constantly looking at the clock only to see ten minutes had passed. I was rarely this anxious at work. It took a lot to rile me up or get me flustered. The woman who was some ten stories down looking over camera footage was one of those things. When it was about ten after one and Coral still had yet to come to return, I called down to Ron's office.

"Hey boss," he answered.

"Ron, is Coral with you?" I asked, bypassing greetings.

"She actually left two minutes ago. We've been looking at footage for hours. I'm not sure if anything was learned." He sounded doubtful.

"Alright. Thanks." Just as I looked up I saw Coral greeting Darlene outside my office. A sigh of relief escaped. "She's here. I'll ask her take on it." I hung up quickly as Coral knocked on my door and entered.

"You don't have to knock, Coral. You're free to enter my office whenever. I ordered your favorite, a honey-glazed salmon salad."

My chest expanded as she smiled in appreciation.

"Thank you. Where are we going after lunch?" she asked as she slid onto the couch, grabbing a fork and the salad.

I found my eyes wandering to toned legs encased in a pair of black leggings, and a pair of brown knee high boots. I watched as she crossed her legs and unfolds a napkin over her lap.

"Li…"

I'm caught.

Our gazes collided and I felt those odd sensations only she elicited rise in the pit of my stomach. I could tell she felt something as well as she quickly removed her gaze from mine and peered down at her salad.

I cleared my throat. "Did you have a question?" I asked, pulling up a chair closer to the low table in front of the couch.

"You said we were going to see a community center? Tell me about it."

"Not yet," I said uncapping a bottle of water and handing it to her. "I want you to see it before I reveal too much."

"Can you tell me how long you've been running it?"

"A little over four and a half years now. It's been around for more than twenty years, but it was in financial turmoil for some time before we took over. When I took over Bennett Industries I wanted to strengthen our social responsibility to the community. Not just improving how we utilize environmental resources but how we treat the people in our community as well."

I noticed Coral pause in between bites to stare at me. I was unable to discern the look but it sent a warm feeling spreading throughout my chest. We ate in a comfortable silence for the remainder of our lunch and a little before two pm we headed down to the building's garage to take a town car to the community center. During the twenty-minute car ride I watched Coral's profile. I was struck by how beautiful she was and how it'd been so long since we were in each other's presence. No other woman had dominated my thoughts the way this woman had for years. I knew from the first moment I saw her that she was going to play a pivotal role in my life and as I sat there trying to discreetly observe her, I knew this to still be the truth. She was the reason for almost every decision I'd made in the last five years.

"Looks like we're here," she said as we pulled up.

I turned to look out the window and noticed we'd arrived at our destination. "So, we are. Come on," I encouraged and pulled her by the hand helping her out of the car. I only released her hand after I felt her tugging for me to let go.

She was already two steps ahead of me heading towards the door. "Well, 'Mr. King of Surprises', show me what you've got here."

I smiled knowing she was trying to maintain her distance from me. I shook my head knowing her strategy is futile. The longer I was in her presence the more I realized this thing between us was undeniable and always had been. I started to rethink my plan of keeping my own distance while I handled this little problem to keep her safe. *Maybe next to me was where she was safest after all,* I wondered as I followed her inside the huge brick building.

As we entered, we were greeted by Ava, one of our part-time interns. "Welcome, Mr. Bennett and Miss Coleman." Ava was a graduate student studying child psychology. Here at the community center she did a lot of our administrative work, as well as leading two child-centered talk groups.

"Coral, this is Ava," I introduced, as Ava began telling Coral all about our facilities.

"Here we have state-of-the-art computers and technology for the kids to do their homework, research projects, or just use at their leisure. Each child is given a maximum of three hours per week that they can be on the computer or tablet, because as important as technology is, we also like to stress physical activity. Many of our kids go to schools that have cut gym classes and recess, so we like to give them time here to run around and exert some of that pent up energy." Ava continued to talk as we moved from the classroom area where the technology was to the side of the center that housed our gymnasiums and pool. "Here we have the smaller gymnasium where our basketball team practices."

"Your center has its own basketball team?" Coral asked, as she shifted her gaze between me and Ava.

"Oh yes, we have basketball, volleyball, baseball and track & field teams that play against other community centers throughout the area." Ava winked at Coral. "We're the Scorpions," Ava announced, taking pride in the team's name.

Coral abruptly turned towards me. "The Scorpions?"

"Yes, Mr. Bennett changed the name when his company took ownership of the center. All the kids love the name," Ava answered unaware of the significance behind the name.

"Liam?" she questioned, her voice full of confusion.

"I'll take over the tour from here, Ava. I know you have group in a few minutes. Thank you for your time."

"No problem, Mr. Bennett. It was nice meeting you, Coral."

"Same here," Coral responded, before turning back to me. "Why did you name your center's sports team that?"

I placed my hand at the small of her back. "Come on," I urged, avoiding her question. "There's more to show."

I escorted her down the hall where we had other after school classes going on. I showed her into the rooms where we held ballet classes three days a week and another where we have a trained martial artist come in and teach the kids Karate and other self-defense moves. There were also art classes and writing classes. In a separate building from the main one, we held nutrition classes for older kids and adults, parenting classes, computer classes, and résumé and career development courses for adults who want to turn their life around. This community center had been one of my proudest accomplishments and it was because of the woman next to me, staring in awe at the scene around us.

"Have you figured out why I changed the team name?" I asked as we ended our tour in the larger gymnasium where our basketball team made up of 9-11 year olds prepared for a scrimmage.

"Our trip to New York?" she asked.

I nodded. During our sophomore year Coral and I took our first trip to New York together. It was just a weekend getaway on one of our long weekends, when neither of us wanted to go back home. We often spent our school breaks with one another. During that first trip, Coral took me back to the Bronx neighborhood where she grew up. We visited the community center where she learned boxing and her sister first took ballet lessons. She spent many hours at that center avoiding going home to an alcoholic, abusive father. She told me how that community center felt more like home than her actual home did. There she learned self-defense, which she used to not only protect herself, but Stacey as well. Unfortunately, a year after our visit the community center closed down due to the city's budget cuts. Coral was devastated. For someone like myself who grew up in the lap of luxury and never having to wonder about getting enough food or being able to afford extracurricular activities, it was life-altering to see how some children struggled. She opened my eyes to a lot and I wanted to pay her back in some small way. So, one of the first things I did after taking over Bennett Industries was to take over and run this community center. As long as our company was still in business, this community center would never have to worry about shutting down, and Bennett Industries wasn't going anywhere.

"Yeah," I answered. "I know it's a little morbid to name our athletic teams after my best friend's codename, but if it wasn't for said friend, this community center would no longer exist." I looked down into her eyes. That chemistry that always existed between us came back and neither one of us wanted to look away.

Finally, Coral turned her head to look down onto the court from the bleachers. "Who runs the center during the day while you're at Bennett Industries?" she asked.

I grinned seeing the man of the hour enter the gymnasium. I'd known him for close to a decade now and I didn't think I'd trust anyone else with the running of this center.

"Here he comes now," I said, at the same time nudging Coral's leg and tilted my head in his direction. I waited for her response, and she didn't disappoint.

"Holy shit," she said out loud. She turned gawking at me. "Are you serious?"

I tilted my head and shrugged my shoulders as Brian approached us.

"You gonna sit up in them bleachers and gawk or get down here and say hello?" he asked, laughing at Coral.

"Brian Simmons! Oh my God!" she exclaimed, standing and rushing down the bleachers.

I followed and watched as they embraced. Brian served with us in Iraq. He fell under Coral's command for a period of time before an injury sent him stateside. It took a while for him to rehab, but four years ago when I was looking for someone to run the community center full-time I knew I could trust Brian while I waited for the person I really wanted to take over to arrive.

"What are you doing here?" Coral asked Brian.

"Working. And you? It's been so long," he stated, still holding onto her waist.

My fingers itched to pull them apart. I was man enough to admit I was a little peeved that Coral's reaction to Brian was a lot more receptive than her initial reaction to me the previous day. Of course, she had just overheard me telling Jeremy to send her back home.

"Tell me about it. How are you?" she asked, finally stepping back to eye him.

"I'm great. It was a long road back, but this guy," he said, tilting his head toward me, "definitely helped."

"I didn't do anything. You've helped me more than the other way around," I commented.

"I highly doubt that. Anyway Scorpion, what have you been up to?"

Coral shrugged. "A little of this a little of that."

Brian nodded knowingly. "You're both staying for the game right? It's just a scrimmage, but the kids are excited about it."

"Of course we are," Coral answered.

We all sat back down in the bleachers and Coral and Brian talked about the team and more about the community center. She asked a ton of questions including what his future plans were at the center and how many kids came in on a daily basis. Their conversation flowed easily, leaving me feeling like the odd man out. I reminisced on the days where Coral and I could talk for hours about everything and about nothing at the same time. I want to get back to that place. I wanted to make her understand why I did what I did, but there was hesitation on my part. Not only would my secrets place her in more danger, but there was a lot about my life that had changed in the last few years. She didn't know everything about me anymore and that scared the shit out of me.

Coral turned to me as we exited the community center an hour later. "Thank you for bringing me here. It's wonderful what you and Brian are doing here, Li."

My chest expanded at how easily she had fallen into using my nickname. A nickname I actually hated until she used it.

"Are the financial records for the community center kept on the same books as Bennett Industries?" she inquired as we began the drive back to my office.

"Not quite. Bennett Industries owns the community center as a subsidy and Brian has an accountant on staff and bookkeeper to do all their recordkeeping. We keep everything as separate as possible, except during tax season. Do you think there could be a link between what Larry found and the community center?"

A contemplative look crossed her face. "I'm not sure. Just want to check every angle. I looked at hours of footage earlier today with Ron and didn't find anything too suspicious. We're going to start setting up interviews."

"Sounds good," I agreed.

We talked about how the interviews will go over the next few weeks, and Coral's plan to have Ron interview most of the staff one on one, while she watched from a separate room. I could tell from the way she talked about it, she believed someone inside the company had something to do with Larry's death, and I was inclined to believe it as well. That pissed me off thinking someone on my payroll could betray the company, and fellow colleagues, in this way.

"I'm going to kick the ass of whoever's involved in this," I said, squeezing my fist tightly.

"Down, boy," Coral teased, patting my clenched fist. "We need to be smart about this. We can get to the ass kicking later."

Her hand on mine had a soothing effect. While my anger didn't disappear, it was put on the back burner for now.

Coral began to gather her things once we entered my office. "I'll have to check the community center out again before this case is over and I leave."

The air left my lungs at the thought of her leaving. I might not have expected her to be there so soon, but now that she was I couldn't imagine her not being there either.

"We'll begin the interviews tomorrow," she continued.

I nodded, opting to remain silent as her business-like facade returned. The more laid back attitude of earlier was beginning to disappear and she was now putting her guard up. I didn't like it.

"You know, you don't have to rush out so soon. We can order an early dinner and catch up," I said, shrugging nonchalantly. I tried to play casual, but I felt anything but.

"Catch up?" A perfectly arched eyebrow raised.

I smirked. "Yeah, you know, talk like regular people. Friends, even."

"Li, I appreciated seeing the community center and even the gesture of you naming the athletic team after me, but we don't have much to talk about outside this case."

"I disagree." The lower register of my voice took on a seductive tone as I moved closer to her. I pulled her leather jacket out of her grasp and tossed it back onto the couch. "We have a lot to talk about," I nearly growled, pulling her by the waist into my arms, and caressing her cheek with my thumb. I saw a vein in her neck pulse alerting me to the fact that she was not immune to my touch.

"I..." She stopped, lowered her head and shaking it as if trying to break out of a trance. I could feel her try to step out of my embrace, but I tightened my grasp.

I placed a finger under her chin, raising it to force her to look at me. "There's a lot you don't know. I would have never left if it weren't for a good reason," I said, and brought my lips down to hover just above hers. Just as our lips were about to touch, I heard my door burst open.

"Daddy!" A pint-size ball of energy shrieked as she sprinted towards me. Instinctively, I stepped back from Coral and stretched my arms wide to scoop her up. I stared down into the face that looked so much like mine.

"Hi, Daddy!" Laura excitedly exclaimed. Her nanny, Anna, wasn't far behind.

"I'm sorry, she couldn't wait to see you," Anna apologized. I looked from Anna to Coral who was now staring wide-eyed at me.

"Oh, you must be in a meeting. We can come back," Anna started, but was interrupted by Coral.

"No, we're done here," she said abruptly, grabbed her bag and jacket, and made a beeline for the door.

"Coral!" I yelled to her back but she didn't even break stride. "Dammit!" I cursed. This was damn sure not how I wanted Coral to find out I was a father.

CHAPTER 8

*L*iam is a father. Liam has a daughter. A daughter who is a spitting
image of her father.

Those thoughts kept spinning around and around as I
continued my run around Bachman Lake Park.

After running out of Li's office, I headed straight to my hotel
room, threw on some workout clothes, and went down to the hotel's
gym. As I used some of the weights to do a circuit workout, I kept
picturing Liam holding that little girl in his arms as if it was the most
natural thing in the world. I wondered if that was the reason he'd up
and left me, because he found out Michele was pregnant with his
child? But even as I contemplated that, the timing didn't make sense.
That little girl looked to be no older than three years old, and Li had
married Michele close to six years ago. And speaking of Michele,
where the hell was she? Just yesterday, Li had said that he was no
longer married.

Even during my sweaty circuit workout I couldn't get my brain to
slow down, so instead of going back to my hotel room, I opted to go
for a run. I checked the pedometer on my arm and realize I was
nearing mile five. I decided to run one more mile before stopping to
stretch and head back to the hotel. Questions about Liam and his

daughter continued to invade my thoughts. I'd kept a lid on my feelings for him for so long and seeing him with his child felt like ripping a Band-Aid off an old, but unhealed wound. I didn't even realize I was clutching my lower abdomen as I sat in my car thinking of Liam being a father. I closed my eyes and counted to ten as thoughts of "what ifs" made their way to the surface. I shook my head, refusing to allow myself to go there. It'd been years and I would not look back. Liam's life was here without me. I would solve this case, figure out who Ghost was, take care of him and go back to Savannah.

It didn't escape me that I didn't refer to Savannah as home. I didn't know any place that had ever felt truly like home, not since my mother died. Savannah was close, but it was a place where I rested, not exactly where I comfortably slept.

I reached my hotel suite and slid the key card in, carrying my gym bag over my shoulder. As soon as I entered the door, the hairs on the back of my neck stood up. I was immediately on high alert. I quickly reached into my gym bag, pulled out my glock nineteen, and quietly placed the bag on the floor. I did a quick scan of the living room and saw everything was as I'd left it. Still, I knew someone else was there.

I turned right towards the bedroom, letting my gun lead the way. As soon as I nudged the door open, I spotted a pair of black oxfords. I recognized the shoes, but I didn't lower my gun even as I raised my gaze and allowed my eyes to rake over his entire body. His green eyes glared at me as he sat comfortably on the edge of the bed.

"Are you trying to get yourself killed?" I asked, sarcastically.

"You weren't going to shoot without knowing who it was," Liam answered, completely unbothered.

"How did you get into my room?"

"I own the hotel." That cocky attitude made me want to smack that half smirk off his face. "You gonna lower the gun?" he asked, standing and staring at the glock still aimed directly at him.

It was my turn to smirk. "I'll think about it."

"Coral."

"What do you want, Li?"

"We need to talk."

"You said that earlier and my answer still stands. We d—"

"Bullshit." He cut me off taking a step closer.

"Alright, you want to talk. Let's talk. How old is your daughter?"

"She's almost three."

"What's her name?"

"Laura."

"After your grandmother," I mumbled, but he still heard me.

"Yes, I named her after my grandmother."

"Where is her mother? You said you were no longer married."

I watched as Liam visibly swallowed and lowered his lashes briefly. "Michele died of a brain aneurysm a month after giving birth."

I closed my eyes in a moment of sadness for the little girl who'd lost her mother before she was old enough to have any memory of her. Before I could open my eyes fully, I felt Liam snatch the gun from my grip. I watched as within less than three seconds, he released the magazine, popped the one remaining bullet out of the chamber, and tossed my now useless weapon to the floor. I forgot how damn quick he was as he grabbed both of my arms by the wrists and hoisted them above my head, pushing me back against the wall with his big body.

"Let. me. go." I seethed.

"No," he growled just as angry. "You're too goddamn stubborn for your own good."

"I have a damn right to be!" I yelled in his face. "You told me you loved me and then you ran off and married someone else and started a whole family." My anger propelled me to ask the question I've wanted to know all these years. "What the hell is that!?"

"I didn't start a family."

I simply eyed him like he had lost his mind. "You have a kid with her Liam."

He sighed. "Just fucking listen. I married Michele not because I wanted to, but for reasons I can't get into. I was miserable. She knew our marriage was a sham. We hardly lived together the whole two years we were married. It was a marriage for show. One night I was feeling lonely and missing my best friend. One thing lead to another. We had s—"

I cut him off. "Please spare me the details on how you fucked your wife, Li."

"Dammit, Coral. She and I were only together that one night and Laura is the product. I didn't mean for....but she's here and she's mine."

I saw the tenderness in his eyes when he mentioned his daughter. It tugged at something deep within me and I felt drawn to him, but I refused to let him see it. I turned my head to look away from him. He was too close. His body pressed up against mine. His familiar scent. All invading my senses. Senses that are were too vulnerable right now.

"Fine. You said what you had to. You can leave now," I said, trying to free my wrists from his hold, but he only tightened the vice grip he had.

"Look at me." His voice was low and the command made my nipples harden.

I silently prayed he couldn't see them through my thin nylon shirt and sports bra.

"Look at me, CeCe."

Damn. Hearing my nickname on his lips like this sent my lower lips pulsating. I turned my head to look up at him.

"I never loved Michele. Everything I told you in Savannah that night was the God's honest truth." He lowered his head and his lips grazed the column of my neck, before he nipped my earlobe. The move sent warmth spreading throughout my entire body. I bit my lower lip to keep from moaning out loud. I didn't want to give him the satisfaction.

"You should go," I protested, but the words sounded weak to my own ears.

"I don't have to be an expert in body language and facial expressions to know you don't want me to go." He slid his free hand up my nylon covered thigh and moved over to cup my mound.

"Li," I said in a voice that sounded strangely like a moan.

"I've missed the hell out of you, CeCe."

"Don't call me that."

This asshole had the nerve to chuckle. A serious curse out was on the tip of my tongue, but before I could get the first word out, he covered my lips with his own. The softness of his lips was a contradiction to the hardness of his kiss. Liam didn't waste time feeling out the kiss. He pressed his lips to mine, demanded entrance and then used his tongue to explore my mouth. As soon as our tongues touched, the sensations went straight to my core, and caused my already damp panties to become even wetter. The logical part of me told me to push him away and move from his embrace, but when his hand moved underneath my shirt, pushed my sports bra aside, and tweaked my hard nipples, I could no longer think straight.

Slowly, Liam loosened his grip on my wrists, but continued to press my body into the wall with his body weight. I aimed to wrap my arms around his neck to get even closer, but he pulled back before I could. Impatiently, he pulled my shirt over my head along with my bra, and tossed both to the floor. When he lowered his head and swirled his tongue around one erect nipple, the groan that escaped my mouth was the only sound that could be heard in the room. I pushed my chest towards his hungry mouth, encouraging him to suck harder. He happily obliged. He released my left nipple with a loud "pop" and moved to the right one.

"Liam, I need to touch you," I practically begged, needing to feel his skin against mine. Any pretense of not wanting to be this close to him flew out the window.

He lifted his face from my breasts. "Then touch me," he directed, right before he pressed his lips to mine again.

With my hands free, I began unbuttoning his shirt, and slid it and his Armani suit jacket down his strong biceps. I felt goosebumps rise along his arms as my fingers moved over them. I attempted to lean back to stare at his bared chest, but Liam swooped down and hoisted me up by the legs, causing me to wrap my legs around his waist. He strolled over to the bed and seconds later, I felt the plush sheets kissing my back as he came down on top of me. He leaned back on his knees in between my legs and stared down at me. My eyes fell from his face down to his large chest. I smiled, seeing the Texas flag tattoo. I reached up to trace the flag with my finger, remembering going with him to the tattoo parlor on his twenty-first birthday to get it done.

My gaze moved lower and I saw the four-inch scar that began from the left side of his upper abdomen and nearly reached his belly button. I ran my finger along the ragged, raised edges of the scar, also remembering the fateful day this happened. I closed my eyes, remembering exactly how intertwined our histories were. His body literally told the story of us.

"Look at me," he commanded, hovering over me.

Slowly, I opened my eyes to stare into his which darkened with passion so much so they almost looked black.

"I never left. You were always right here," he said at the same time he lifted my hand to cover his heart. "If you don't believe anything else, believe that." He held my hand to his heart, leaned down, and kissed me again.

I moaned into his mouth as his thickening erection pressed into my center. I didn't know what to believe in that moment, but I knew I wanted to feel more of him. Even if it was just for the time being. Liam must have felt the same too, because he released my mouth, pulled back and began pulling my running leggings and thong down. He moved quickly, removing my sneakers and the rest of my clothing, discarding them somewhere on the floor. When he lowered his head, it was then I remembered I'd just come back from a sweaty run. I pressed my hand to his shoulder to stop him.

"Liam, I just got finished running. Maybe we should do this in the shower," I said, rising to move. I was stopped by his hands around my waist.

"Don't move." He glared at me and lowered his face to my quivering pussy lips.

I thought he was going to put his mouth on me, but instead he moved in closer with his nose and inhaled deeply.

"Mmm. *For five years*, I've only had the memory of your scent. You're not going anywhere." He groaned as he inhaled me again and then began tonguing my clit.

"You're so damn nasty," I said around a moan as I plopped back down against the bed. "Oooh," I moaned as his tongue began making circular motions around my engorged clit. I felt his lips kiss my labia and his grip around my waist tightened as he pulled me even further into him. I couldn't keep still. This felt too good and I wanted more. I began pushing my hips up and moving my pelvis in a circular motion.

"That's it, baby. Fuck my face," he growled, seconds before he pulled me even closer to his mouth. His tongue lashed even more quickly against my clit and his lips slapped and slurped up my juices.

It felt so good my back arched off the bed. "Liam, what are you doing to me?" I moaned.

"I'm writing my name on this pussy." It's then he pressed his tongue hard against my clit and I came apart. "Oooh, shiiit!" I yelled as the most wonderful sensations overtook me. I hadn't felt that good in a long time. I was still trying to catch my breath, only for it to be snatched again when I felt Liam's stiff thickness push into me. I felt every inch and ridge as he filled me up, maintaining eye contact the whole time. He used his eyes and body to tell me what his mouth already did. I felt overwhelmed, overcome with emotions that I've only felt for this man. I turned to look away, but he used his hand to cup my neck and chin.

"Don't you dare. Look at me," he ordered and shifted his hips to move in a rhythm that had my pussy singing his praises. He didn't immediately pound into me, instead he took long, measured strokes to allow me adjust to his girth.

"More, Li. I need more," I begged.

The cocky smirk he gave me caused my pussy to flood even more. He picked up the pace, using his free hand to pull my leg around his waist. He began pumping into me even faster, while moving his hand to massage my clit.

"Oh, God!" I gasped.

"That feel good, baby?"

"Yesss," I hissed, raising my hips to meet his heavy strokes.

"Five fucking years, I've been missing this," he pushed into me with each word. He lowered his face to mine and kissed my lips, then removed his hand and began sucking on the sensitive column of my neck.

I wrapped my arms around his broad shoulders and pulled him

even closer. By now, he was pounding me into the mattress and it felt like heaven. I raised my other leg to wrap around his hip and secured them around his waist. I pushed the back of my head into the pillows, granting him better access to my neck. He continued to suck and moved his hands under my ass, raising me up. With every stroke, he hit my G-spot. My vaginal walls started fluttering and I knew another orgasm was just seconds away.

"Li, I'm about to come."

"Come for me, CeCe. Let me see it." He pulled back to look into my face.

The passion filled expression on his face sent me over into oblivion. I clenched my pussy around his thrusting cock and my second orgasm flooded my whole body with euphoria. I knew he wanted to see me come so I struggled to keep my eyes open watching him as he watched me. My orgasm must have triggered his and soon after he threw his head back and the vein at the side of his neck bulged, at the same time I felt him release inside of me. He continued to pound and thrust until the last tremors of his orgasm subsided. I finally closed my eyes and tried to control my breathing. I felt him above me as he pulled out and moved to my side. The sense of loss was immediate, but I pushed it away. Slowly, my common sense returned and I realized what had just happened between us. My eyes sprung open and I saw Liam watching me. Without a word, I hopped out of the bed and stormed into the bathroom, slamming the door behind me.

I locked the door and pressed my back against it, covering my face with my hand. "What the hell did I just do?" I murmured to myself. I let my hands glide down my face and turned to stare in the mirror. My hair looked tousled, and I noticed red marks forming on my breasts and neck where Li sucked my skin. Despite my brown complexion even minor bruising tended to show up easily. The marks and the throbbing between my legs reminded me of exactly what had happened. I sighed deeply and ran my hand through my messy, short curls. I grabbed the robe hanging on the door and made a decision.

I cinched the robe securely at my waist before stepping out of the bathroom door. I nearly walked right into Li who was standing at the bathroom doorway, and I had to tamp down the urge to beg him to take me again. The hard set of his jaw and his closeness told me he was determined to not let what just happened go.

"CeCe," he called and the passion in his voice made my belly quiver.

I ignored him and squeezed past to the bedroom entrance, stooping to pick up his shirt and suit jacket. I tossed his clothing in his direction. "It's time for you to go."

"What?"

"You heard me. It's time for you to go." I moved to the opposite side of the bed and found his boxers and pants and tossed those to him as well.

"CeCe—"

"Don't call me that!" I shouted. That damn nickname got under my skin. It was too intimate, and I didn't want to feel close to Liam. I just wanted him to go. "Get dressed so you can go."

"You can't just kick me out."

"Why the hell not?"

"Goddammit, Ce—"

I gave him a murderous look.

"Coral, just talk to me." By then, he was putting his boxers back on.

I refused to even look at him, knowing that if I did, I would have fallen back into bed with him, and talking would be the last thing we did.

"No," I said petulantly, shaking my head. "Just go. Now!"

I heard him let off a rant of swearing, but I remained with my back to him until I saw him go to pick up his shoes out of the corner of my eye. I moved to walk past him to the suite door, but his arms caught me around the waist. I was caught off-guard and before I could break out of his hold, he caught my free hand and pushed it around my back, holding us chest to chest.

"Let me go."

"I will. I'll also leave, but this isn't over. You and I are far from over."

"Fuck you, Li," I spit out.

The mischievous smile he gave me caused my belly to quiver all over again. "You just did," he cockily stated before pressing a quick peck to the tip of my nose and releasing me.

I didn't turn around as the door opened and closed. I felt the loss of him as he exited. I closed my eyes and counted down from ten to one, trying to regain some sort of control over my wayward emotions. Part of me wanted to run back to him and ask him to comeback. The other part wanted to kick his ass for stirring up all this shit I worked hard to bury. I hated feeling so out of control.

I opened my eyes and walked back into the bedroom. I sat on the bed and tried to talk myself out of chasing Li down. I wouldn't do it. I stood and began picking up my discarded clothes and the pieces of my disarmed gun. Once I put all that away, I called down to the hotel's maid service and requested a fresh pair of bed sheets and pillow cases. There was no way I could lay my head down in this bed with Liam's scent all over it. It took less than ten minutes before the sheets were delivered, after which I changed the sheets and then prepared to shower. I knew I wouldn't be getting much sleep tonight, but what else was new?

* * *

Liam

This stubborn ass woman.

A whole damn week had passed since she kicked me out of her hotel room. Imagine that. She kicked me out of a damn hotel that I own. Technically, Jeremy owned that portion of the company, but I still signed off on the financials. For the last week, she'd been working with Ron to get through the employee interviews and so far nothing had turned up. She'd done everything in her power to not be alone with me, or avoid me altogether. However, I'd finally figured out how to get her alone.

My phone rang loudly, interrupting my thoughts.

"Yes."

"Mr. Bennett, your father is on line one."

The scowl on my face was instant. He was the last person I wanted to talk to. Ever. He usually called in to check in on the business while he was in Austin. I provided him minimal information, so there was a lot he didn't know. Over the last few years, I've had a team digging into his history to get all the dirt on him.

"Put him through," I told my secretary.

"Hello, son. How is business going?"

Straight to business. That was my old man. Didn't stop to ask about me or his granddaughter. He was a son of a bitch, but most people didn't know that about him. He painted a perfect image for the outside world, but behind closed doors, it was a different story.

"Hello, Richard. Business is business."

I started calling him by his first name years ago. My father enjoyed the money and prestige that came with being the CEO of such a large and well-respected company, and even the influence, but he wanted more. Hence, his current position.

"Yes, well, speaking of business, I'm not sure if I agree with all the time and money you're putting into these alternative energies. Our family has thrived for three generations off of oil and now you're trying to change it up. I'm speaking with some big oil companies this week about investing in the pipeline. I'm going to suggest Bennett Industries be an investor in this pipeline as well. The payoff will be huge. And you have Jeremy expanding the hotel side. I told you I don't like that bastard nephew of mine."

I closed my eyes and pinched the bridge of my nose to hold off my irritation. "We've been over this. The pipeline has a lot of problems and the future of energy is in alternative energies, not fossil fuels. Bennett Industries will be ahead of the curve with these energies we are working on. And Jeremy is running his end of the business with great success. His involvement in Bennett Industries is not up for discussion. You're a busy man and I'm sure you have work to do as do I. Bye," I said, before hanging up.

I knew that seemed harsh, but most had no idea who that man was. He spent my entire childhood chastising my mother and me then pasting on a smile when we were out in public. I was a bastard before

Coral, and well, it was because of him. I watched him do some very unscrupulous things to remain on top, including screwing business rivals' wives. And that was not even the worst of it.

My father's call did remind me to have my assistant make a few phone calls for my upcoming Austin trip. I knew exactly the businesses my father wanted Bennett Industries to work with on this pipeline, but instead of the pipeline, I'd been working to convince them to invest in our alternative energies. Before I left my office, I told my assistant to set up a trip for me to go to Austin for a few days to meet with the same businessmen. Once that was done, I rose from my chair and stretched, preparing to pop in on the woman who'd been avoiding me for a damn week.

* * *

I WALKED into the security office and found the object of my affections closely watching the large flat screen monitor hanging from the wall. I watched her profile and noted how intently she was watching the scene in front of her. I glanced at the screen to see Ron in another room interviewing Mikhail from marketing and sales. I looked back at Coral, noting her flawless skin and the column of her neck. My fingers twitched with the need to touch the soft skin and feel her tremble underneath them.

"Stop staring," she said, keeping her gaze on the screen.

My lips kicked up into a half smile. "I can't help it." My voice was slightly deeper than usual. She made me feel all types of shit.

Without looking at me, she asked, "Liam, what are you doing here?"

"Last time I checked, I run this company and can go anywhere I damn well please." My eyebrow raised. My words had come out harsh. Her refusal to even acknowledge my presence pissed me off. Do you know how angering it was to be in the same room with the woman you've wanted for more than a decade, and she wouldn't even look at you? The same woman, I might add, who'd been screaming my name at the top of her lungs just a week ago.

Finally, she turned to me, rolling her eyes.

"Whatever," she spat before turning back to the monitor, effectively dismissing me.

Not today. "We need to talk."

"No, we don't."

"Like hell we don't," I growled, losing my composure.

"Li, this isn't a damn game," she retorted angrily, turning her whole body to face me. "I did not come here to play whatever game you're playing. Your employee is dead and someone in your company may very well be responsible for it. Your other employees could be in danger. *You* could be in danger. Now, is not the time to play around!"

She huffed, now standing. That pissed me off even more.

I moved closer to her. "First of all, let's get one thing clear; don't ever imply that I don't care about my employees. I care very much that Larry may have been killed because of this company. That is why I actually called Jabari to have him look up any aliases Larry may have had. Turns out, he did and he had a safe deposit box, which housed his laptop. I didn't need to visit his fiancée."

"You have his laptop?" she asked, cutting me off.

"Yes, and your stubborn ass would have had it this morning when I requested you visit my office, if you hadn't been avoiding me. These are my employees." I pointed to my chest. "I am responsible for every single one and I do not take that lightly. You of all people should know exactly how serious I take my responsibilities as a leader," I finished, reminding her of the time we served together. I might have been many things—cocky, arrogant, even a showboat when the occasion arises, but I was a damn good leader and those who worked under me were my team and I made sure to look after them.

Those hazel eyes stared at me for a few seconds, taking in what I'd said. When she bowed her head slightly, I knew she was contrite. "You're right. I didn't mean to imply that you didn't care."

She sighed, running a hand through her short curls. She turned back to the screen, but the look in her eyes just before she turned gave me pause. I know Coral. We spent years getting to know each other as best friends. She didn't let many people in, but she did let her guard down around me eventually. I noticed her body language as she peered at the screen, watching Ron and Mihkail. In that moment, I had a realization and it caused the hair at the back of my neck to stand up.

"Wait a minute," I said out loud, staring at her.

She turned, looking back at me, but remained silent.

"This is deeper than Larry or Bennett Industries. You're worried. Why?" I asked, stepping even closet, and gripping her elbow.

She didn't pull back, but her response was not what I wanted either. "I don't know what you're talking about."

"Don't give me that shit. This is personal for you for some reason. I mean, outside of it just involving me. What is it?" I knew she was holding something back. I felt it. I've developed a sixth sense for this woman. I could feel this case held something deeper for her.

"It's nothing." She stepped away from me just as Ron entered the room.

"Interviews do—oh, Liam. I didn't know you were watching," he said.

"I thought I'd stop by and see how things are going," I said to Ron, but still hadn't taken my eyes off Coral.

"Well, it looks like Mihkail's all clear. He didn't know anything about what Larry had been working on. Nor, did he speak with Larry in the days before his death. I'm starting to think this is a waste of time. None of these employees have demonstrated any signs they're lying," Ron continued.

Coral's head spun to look at Ron and by the face she gave him, I already know where this was headed. "You sure about that?" she asked.

She wasn't the best at what she did for nothing. She read people a hell of a lot better than Ron ever could.

Ron shrugged. "Yeah. He didn't hesitate in answering most of my questions and looked me in the eye when answering. He's fine, as are most of the employees."

"He's lying," Coral announced, matter-of-factly.

"What? Did you not just hear what I said? He looked me right in the eye and answered where he was the night Larry died."

"Ron, let her finish," I interjected, not liking the rising level of his voice. "If she says he was lying then he was lying," I stated confidently.

She looked at me and for the briefest second, her eyes softened before shifting to Ron. "Look here," she insisted grabbing the remote and pressing a button to bring Ron's four interviews onto the screen. Mihkail's interview was in the bottom right corner.

"You asked him where he was the night of Larry's death. He looked you right in the eye and said he had dinner with a client. He named the restaurant and everything. Same here." She paused to press a button and the interview with Suzanne, an accountant, came up as Ron asked the same question. "Suzanne looks you in the eye and said she was home watching television."

"Yeah and?"

"And, they're lying."

"How do you know?" Ron questioned.

"We've been told you look someone in the eye when you're telling the truth. That's actually not true. When people tell the truth, they need to recall events that happened. They will look down and to the left. Not because they're lying, but because they're trying to remember. People who look you right in the eye on purpose are trying to convince you they're telling the truth *because* they're lying. Plus, they gave you way too many details—details you didn't ask for. Suzanne gave you the names of characters from the cable program, Mihkail told you, down to the dessert what he ate at the restaurant. Too many details is another sign someone is trying to *convince* you they're telling the truth, *not actually* telling the truth. Mihkail and Suzanne both lied. In fact, at some point in each interview everyone lied."

"So, you're saying everyone I interviewed could have been involved in this?" Ron asked.

Coral shook her head. "No, everyone lies about something. It's just determining what they're lying about. Look at Mihkail, while he's looking you in the eye, he's twisting his wedding band with his right hand. Sign of guilt. And Suzanne, when you move on to another question, for a nanosecond her lips thin and pull back into the universal look of shame." Coral paused the frame and sure enough Mary's lips were pulled into a thin line. It was a minute expression that most would have missed, but not Coral.

"Suzanne's ashamed of lying. Well, not lying, but what she lied about. She wasn't home watching television that night."

"So, Mihkail and Mary had something to do with Larry's death?" Ron asked, sounding confused.

Again, Coral shook s her head. "No, when you asked if they knew anything about what he was working on or his death, they were truthful."

"Then why would they lie about where they were that night?" Ron asked.

I could guess what Coral was going to say.

"That's difficult to say. I can tell you whether or not someone is lying, but not necessarily what they are lying about. My guess would be that Mihkail is having an affair. He probably did have a business dinner that night and cut it short to meet his mistress. That's what the twirling his ring was about. He felt guilty. And Suzanne," she pointed the remote at the screen, "…is probably his mistress. That's where her shame comes from of where she was that night."

I sat back in my seat just staring at the screen. "So Mary and Mihkail are having an affair with one another?" I said in amazement.

Coral shrugged. "Probably, but at least they didn't kill Larry. How about we go look at that laptop," she suggested, looking over at me.

I simply nodded and stood. I smirked as I looked over at Ron. He was shocked by what Coral revealed about people he'd worked with for years. In minutes, she'd picked up on what he hadn't in years of working around them. I would have told him not to feel bad about it, but in that moment, I was more concerned with getting Coral up to my office.

I held the door open for her. "We'll look at more interviews tomorrow," Coral turned to tell Ron.

CHAPTER 9

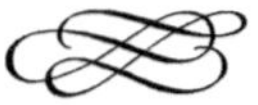

oral

"That was quite a show you put on up there," Liam stated behind me as we entered his office.

"It wasn't a show. Just what I saw," I told him as I sat in what had become my usual spot in his office.

I worked hard the past week not to be alone with him, but I should have known it was inevitable. I was working for the man for the unforeseeable future. I wouldn't be able to avoid him altogether. My head was still messed up from what happened in my hotel room a week ago. Instead of sleepless nights wondering who was trying to kill me, I tossed and turned wanting to feel his touch again. There had been nights, even when I did manage to sleep for a little bit, where I'd wake up to find my fingers in between my legs with a mind of their own, trying to recreate that feeling I had with only him. I sighed, recalling how I had awakened that morning— moaning Liam's name as I brought myself to climax, yet still left unsatisfied.

"I know that you don't put on a show for anyone," he acknowledged, looking me directly in the eye.

His heated gaze warmed me to my core, and was the reason that

I'd been avoiding him. Before last week, I could do my best to ignore the chemistry between us, but it had become undeniable.

"Where's the laptop?" I asked.

"I have it locked away. I'll get it in a sec," he said, casually checking his watch as if I was wasting his time. He stepped behind his desk, slid his hands in his pockets, and stared at me. The look he gave me warmed my entire body. Standing behind his huge desk, in front of his wall length book shelf projecting the very image of power, arrogance and I—no, I didn't even guess that last part.

"Come here," he demanded interrupting my thoughts.

The deep, low command sent shivers down my spine and my nipples began tingling. I looked down at my phone, refusing to acknowledge the hold he had over me.

"Come here, Coral," he repeated, low but with more bass in his voice.

"No." My nipples hardened almost to the point of being painful. I took a chance and looked up into his darkened eyes.

He remained standing behind his huge desk looking like a king atop his throne, his eyes devouring me. "Why not?"

"I'm quite comfortable where I am, thank you. Besides, I need to be leaving soon."

"Bullshit. Come here." He sat in his leather chair and crossed his hands in his lap, just like the arrogant son of a bitch he was.

I became angered at the power he had over my body without even touching me. "Fuck you, Li."

He chuckled. "What did I tell you the last time you said that?"

A throbbing between my legs began as I remembered his exact words and the way he took me just moments after I told him to go fuck himself in my hotel room. I bit my lower lip and squeezed my thighs together, resisting the urge to shift and cross my legs. I didn't want him to see how much he affected me.

"Why are you acting like you don't want me?"

I swallowed deeply and looked him straight in the eye. "Because I don't."

"Liar."

Of course it was a lie, but I refused to admit that to him.

"You're so full of yourself. How do you know I'm lying?"

"Because I can see your nipples straining through your shirt, and I can smell your arousal all the way over here," he said, devouring me with his gaze.

At that point I crossed my legs, squeezed my thighs together even more, but still refused to give in.

"Liar." I told him turning the tables on him.

"Am I?" He raised his brow with a cocky smirk. "Bring your ass over here."

I wanted to hold up my resistance, but I couldn't. His deep voice, arrogant demeanor, and hungry eyes had my body moving on its own in his direction. Once I was within arm's length of him, he reached out and wrapped both arms around my waist, pulling me onto his lap. I was barely seated before his lips captured mine. He nibbled at and tasted my lips before pulling back and staring at me. He took in my whole face as if trying to memorize every inch of it. His hand slowly moved up my back to cup the back of my head before fingering the kinky curls on the top.

"I like your hair like this." His voice was a mixture of awe and appreciation. "What made you cut it?" he asked while moving in to place gentle, yet firm kiss along the column of my neck.

I shivered before responding. "Uh, um, I just wanted a change." I stuttered at the feel of his lips on my skin.

"Beautiful either way," he rasped before moving to my lips again.

I was completely taken over by the kiss; so much so, I barely noticed that we'd moved until I felt the hardness of his desk beneath my butt. Liam pulled back from me, and pushed the few files and papers aside. He unbuttoned and unzipped my jeans. It took me another second to realize what he was doing.

"Liam, this is your office," I whispered, looking towards the door.

"Not a problem," he said, pressing a button underneath his desk. I heard a click alerting me that he'd locked the door.

"No one can save you now." The last word was barely out of his mouth before his lips were back on mine, demanding I open for him.

He pressed into me deeper causing my thighs to widen, and pushed me back on his desk. Pulling back, he tugged and pulled on my jeans, lifting me up to bring them down my legs. He stopped once they are at my ankles, too impatient to take my shoes off. He pressed my thighs even further apart with his palms and dove head first into my awaiting wetness.

"Mmmmm," I moaned as my head lolled back onto his desk. The first swipe of his tongue against my labia had me squeezing my eyes and mouth tightly to avoid yelling out in pleasure. I didn't know who was still in the office, but the last thing I wanted was for them to hear my cries of joy. Liam obviously didn't give a shit about any of that as he continued to lap up my juices, swirling his tongue over my engorged clitoris. He put his entire mouth on me as he feasted on my pussy. A second later, I felt an invasion as his finger sunk into my aching core.

"Liiii," I moaned. I opened my eyes and looked down to see his mass of sandy blond hair bobbing up and down between my legs. The sight caused me to grow even wetter. I slid my hand down to grab a hold of his hair, needing to touch some part of him.

"Goddamn, you taste good," he moaned.

"Liam, I'm gonna come," I panted, trying to push his head away in order to stave off the inevitable. Up until then I had refrained from yelling out, but I knew the orgasm that was coming would end that.

Liam's response was to reach up and grip my ass with both hands, pulling me up and bringing my pussy even closer to his face. This man was born to eat pussy and I was grateful to be on the receiving end.

"Ohhh shiiiitt!" I yelled as my orgasm hit me like a tidal wave. Tingles of ecstasy shot through my entire body and I closed my eyes to see stars.

Liam was relentless, however, as he continued to eat me through my orgasm, licking every last drop of my moisture.

"I don't think I need dinner after that." He stood up a few moments later and stared down at me, licking his lips. His hands remained on my thighs and he moved his eyes to my core as if he was contemplating going in for a second round. It was when he bent over and dipped his head that I finally moved.

"Oh hell no," I said, pressing my palm to his chest pushing him back. I quickly sat up, and tried to hop down off his desk with as much tact as possible, but that was hard to do with my panties and jeans down around my ankles. I still felt the aftermath of Liam's mouth between my legs, and my pussy throbbed for more, but I ignored that feeling as I slid my jeans up my legs and turned to pick up my belongings and leave, but I was stopped by a hand on my wrist.

"Have dinner with me."

I raised a skeptical eyebrow, looking up into his eyes. I cocked my head to the side giving him an, "Are you crazy?" look and he merely chuckled again.

"I've missed the hell out of you, CeCe," he said, repeating the same thing he said in my hotel room the week before. I heard something in his voice that I refused to allow myself to contemplate too much.

Then why'd you leave? I wanted to yell out, but I bit my bottom lip to keep from asking. Liam didn't miss the move and lifted his hand to run his thumb across my bottom lip.

"It's just dinner. I'm meeting a client for drinks to discuss some work, but you and I can have dinner right after. I'll bring Larry's laptop."

My eyes widened as I remembered the laptop being the reason that I had come to see him in the first place. I shook my head. "Ever the chess player."

"Always," he confirmed.

"Alright. Just dinner," I said with a forcefulness even I didn't believe.

"Checkmate," he stated, grinning, knowing he'd won this little round. "And maybe you'll tell me the whole reason you're so interested in this case." There was a hint of warning and concern in his voice.

I knew he intended to find out everything I was keeping from him. My stomach dropped as I remembered how tenacious Li could be when it came to getting his way. The lines between personal and professional had clearly been crossed with this case, but I refused to put Li in any more danger possibly. The issue was my problem to solve.

* * *

"Do you mind if we sit at that table?" I asked the waitress, pointing to a table in the corner. From that table I could see every exit and point of entry. The young waitress looked at me and for the briefest moment I saw scorn pass over her face before she plastered on a smile. I know she was taking note of my subpar jeans and blazer. Usually, jeans weren't allowed in The French Room, but I knew entering with Liam Bennett got my wardrobe overlooked.

"Sure," she answered with false cheer.

"Still not sitting with your back to the door, huh?" Liam asked, smiling at me once the waitress had left.

We'd spent the last thirty minutes at the bar's restaurant for Li's work meeting. As usual, I requested a seating that allowed me to see all the entry and exit points. It was the same reason I chose to sit where I did in Li's office. By then we were sitting down for dinner.

"You've gotten lax in your old age," I retorted. "There was a time that you wouldn't have sat with your back to the door either."

"I've gotten lax about some things, but never about others," he replied, staring at me sharply. I knew he was no longer talking about views of restaurant doors, but I chose not to address his underlying meaning.

"Well, I haven't had the luxury of being able to get lax."

Li tilted his head slightly and gave me a serious look, and I realized that was the wrong thing to say. I knew he was going to pounce on my comment.

"Speaking of which, tell me what you're hiding."

"I have no idea what you're talking about. I'm just doing the job I was hired to do."

Li cocked his eyebrow, obviously not believing me. "I know you better than anyone else. Why—"

"You *used* to know me better than anyone else," I said, cutting him off.

"Get the fuck outta here. I can still read you like a book, no matter how much you try and hold back. I know enough to know you spotted every entrance and exit within thirty seconds of entering this restaurant. I know you cross your right leg over your left leg when you're uncomfortable and your left leg over your right leg when you're relaxed. I know you still drink green tea every morning and I know..." he paused, leaning over the table, "...you've awakened every morning for the last week with your fingers stroking your wet pussy lips remembering what it feels like when I'm balls deep inside you. I know that last part because I've had the same problem." He finally sat back in his chair is eyes still on mine, challenging me to deny his words.

I wanted to refute him. To tell him to get over himself, but it took everything in me to stabilize my heart rate and the ache between my legs his words caused. Thankfully, we were soon interrupted by the waitress. At the same time, my phone beeped alerting that I had a text message.

"I'll have the tenderloin of veal..." Li ordered,

I looked down and see a message from Nathaniel:

Nate: *I'm in DC for the next few weeks. Care to come up for a visit. I'll make it worth your while *wiggles eyebrows**

I smirked. Sometimes I wished I could just want something more with Nate.

Me: *I would but I can't.*

I gave a short response because I rarely explained myself to anyone.

Nate: *Are you sure? You're passing up the opportunity to spend time with GQ's Bachelor of the Year.*

That actually caused me to laugh out loud a little. Nate could be very charming and any woman would be lucky to be in his sights. But I was not any woman. I obviously had problems.

Me: *I'm sure. I'm out of town working a case. Maybe next time.*

Nate: *Suit yourself, but I told you I'm not giving up on us.*

I shook my head at that last comment. I hadn't actually seen Nate since the last time I was in DC, but we'd talked a few times and exchanged emails. I exited my text messages and placed my phone on the table and looked up to a pair of scowling, emerald eyes.

"I ordered you the scallops," he informed me, knowing my love of seafood.

"Thank you."

"Who the hell was that?" he asked through clenched teeth.

I didn't repeat myself. Not even to Liam Bennett. "Excuse you?"

"That was Nate wasn't it?" Liam asked, refusing to back down.

"Who is texting me on the phone that *I* pay the bill on is none of *your* business." I didn't know who the hell he thought he was—wait, that was a lie. I knew exactly who he thought he was. He was the same Liam I'd always known.

"You're still talking to him?" he asked as if he didn't even hear what I'd just told him.

I rolled my eyes, exasperated. "Liam, let it go. We're not here to talk about who's texting me. Did you bring Larry's laptop?" I attempted to steer the conversation away from the personal to the professional. This whole situation had gotten away from me. Especially considering what happened in his office earlier and the direction of the discussion before our waitress and Nate interrupted.

"I have it." He sighed. After a few more moments of glaring at me, he finally pulled out the laptop and opened it. "I haven't opened it since I received it this morning," he advised.

It took a little while to figure out Larry's password, which turned out to be his fiancé's birth date. Once in, we looked through his work files. Everything seemed normal until we came across a password protected file. A filed named "Ghost." The hairs at the back of my neck stood on end. But the password used to log into the laptop wasn't working for the "Ghost" file.

We were no closer to gaining access when the waitress brought our dinner. So, we were left to discuss the case as we ate.

"I think I can have Jabari hack into the computer and look into it," I informed Liam as we finished our dinner.

He nodded and pulled out his wallet to pay the bill.

"I should also go down to the scrap yard where Larry's car is and take a look at it."

"You think someone tampered with it?" he asked.

I shrugged. "Not sure, but worth it to take a look for myself."

"I don't want you to go by yourself," he insisted.

I frowned at him. "You know this is my job and I've been in much more dan—"

He held up his hand. "You're not going alone," he said, cutting me off.

"Whatever," I mumbled, as he stood and came over to pull out my chair for me.

We left the restaurant and instead of taking a car back to my hotel, we opted to walk since it was only a few blocks away. We walked in relative silence, with Liam's hand resting at the small of my back, guiding me through the small crowds on the sidewalk. Part of me wanted to tell him move his hand, but in truth, his touch made me feel safe. I hadn't felt this protected in a long time, and it took all my willpower not to lean into him as we walked. We made our way to my suite and I paused and stared at him. "We nee—"

My words were cut off by his lips. I forgot what I was about to say and lost any fight I had. With his hands on my waist, Liam turned our bodies so my back was flat against the door. His lips caressing mine felt so good I lost all awareness of the fact that we were out in the middle of the hallway making out like a couple of teenagers. My hands found their way up his strong arms and broad shoulders and entwined around the back of his neck. I pulled him in closer, and he didn't hesitate. Li bent his knees slightly and pressed his pelvis against my middle, allowing me to feel his growing hardness. I moaned as moisture pooled in my panties for the umpteenth time that day. I struggled to pull back.

"I need to open door," I panted against his lips.

"Hurry up," he growled.

I quickly retrieved the keycard from my pocket and tried to insert it into the door. Unfortunately, my fingers trembled with so much need, that I slipped a few times. I heard Liam chuckle behind me as his fingers plucked the card from my hand. I looked back at him, giving him a scowl. He never took his eyes from mine as he deftly inserted the keycard and pushed the door open.

I stumbled into the hotel suite and turned on the light, only to pull up short. Instinctively, I reached in my bag for my gun. Before I could take the safety off, I felt a strong band around my waist pulling me back. Liam put his big body in front of mine, with a gun of his own in one hand, and his cell in the other.

"Don't move," he warned.

I was irritated as I looked around my disheveled room. Someone had turned over the suite's couch cushions, gone through the desk drawers, overturned papers. That's all I saw as Liam held me behind him with one arm while he called his security team. I heard him tell Ron to get over to the hotel, and to bring extra security. I wanted to see the bedroom and what damage had been done there, but Liam gave me a warning look.

"Don't fucking move, CeCe."

I squinted at him wanting to curse him out, but I was interrupted when two of Liam's security entered the room. They'd been with us, out of sight, since we left his office, but had remained downstairs.

"Check the bedroom. Make sure nobody's here first," Liam ordered the two men. I watched as they entered the bedroom. I heard them opening doors and calling out to make sure the room was empty.

"All clear!" one called as they exited the bedroom.

Finally, Li dropped his arm from around me, allowing me to move freely from behind him. I still had my gun in my hand, safety off, as I looked around the room. I saw minimal damage had been done to the hotel's property. I hadn't left anything pertaining to this case in my hotel room. All my important files are on my tablet that I carry with me wherever I go.

"Not much damage has been done to the hotel's furniture, but some of your clothing has been torn up."

I raised my eyebrows at Liam's words, not even realizing he'd gone into the bedroom to check everything out for himself.

Liam told me what I'd already begun to discern for myself. "Targeting your clothes gives this a personal feel. But it looks like they were looking for something too."

I nodded absentmindedly.

"You're coming home with me."

I snapped my head up staring at him. "What?"

"You heard me. Whoever was in here has it out for you. You'll stay with me. I have high end security. No one's getting in my home. Pack what you can. We'll leave in ten minutes."

He had the damn nerve to go off and talk with security after he made this declaration like I was just going to follow along. There was no way I was going to stay at his house. I did go in the bedroom to pack up the rest of my belongings. I figured I could just get another room, or stay at another hotel.

I walked around the room, taking inventory of everything that had been touched. Again, dresser drawers had been gone through. I knew whatever it was they were looking for, they didn't find it. I wondered what it was they could be looking for. The only people who knew my true purpose for being there were Li, Jeremy, and a few high ranking members of Li's security team. I began to run through my mental rolodex of everyone I'd come in contact with since arriving in Dallas.

"You ready?" I heard from behind me. I looked over my shoulder to see Li's irritated expression. I could tell he was anxious to get me out of there, but he was about to be even more angered by what I was about to say.

"Almost," I answered as I put a few of my salvaged clothes into my suitcase. "But I'm not going home with you," I told him flat out.

His reaction was immediate as his body stiffened and he glared at me. "You don't have a choice."

That got my hackles up. My voice was low as I gritted the words out through clenched teeth. "I don't know who the hell you think you're talking to."

"*I think*," he said calmly—a little too calm, as he slowly stalked over to me. "You are not safe here." He stopped close enough that our fronts were nearly touching. He leaned down, looking me in the eye. "*I think,* someone has found out you're here and are now gunning for you. *I think* that if you had been here when they were things could have gotten very ugly. And I can't allow that."

I raised an eyebrow. "And why not?"

He leaned down, getting right in my face. I noticed the flare of his nostrils indicating he was trying to keep it together. "Because if something were to happen to you I would tear this entire city apart."

The feral, protective look in his eye caused my breath to hitch and a warm feeling to bloom in my chest. My bodily reactions only served to piss me off, however. I took a step back and bumped into the bed behind me. I crossed my arms over my chest in a sign of defiance.

"I'm not going. I'm not going to stay in a home you shared with your wife. I won—"

"She never lived in my home." His voice was low, but he glared at me in the eye.

I crinkled my eyebrows in confusion and tilted my head silently asking for an explanation.

"I've only lived in my home for two years. I started building it a few months after Laura was born. She never lived there." His face softened slightly. I saw the worry plainly in his eyes.

"What about…?" I paused and cleared my throat. "What about your daughter? Won't she be confused?" I'd never even formally met his little girl. The last thing I wanted was to meet her under strenuous circumstances. Liam's eye lids shuttered for the briefest of moments before he raised his hand to palm my cheek. His thumb stroked my chin and lower lip. I forced myself through sheer will, not to lean into his caress.

"I'll tell her the truth. You're a friend who needs help and will be staying with us for a little while. I have five bedrooms in my home. You'll have your own space."

"What about safety?" I asked.

"You will be completely safe. No one will touch you in my home," he said fiercely, stepping closer.

"I mean you and Laura. Are you sure having me stay with you is best?" I paused, poignantly looking around the room, acknowledging that someone had already found my hotel room and trashed it. "Who's to say this person won't come looking for me at your house and try to harm you guys?"

He cupped my face with both hands this time and looks me straight in the eye. "There is no way I'm letting you sleep anywhere but under my roof tonight. Every square inch of my 3.7 acre property is kept under twenty-four hour surveillance. No one will touch you, my daughter, or anyone else in my home. Are we clear?"

"Crystal," I nodded, finally surrendering.

"Let's go," he said, as he bent down to pick my packed suitcase off the floor. "You have your laptop and everything right?" he asked, as we exited the room.

"Yes, I have everything," I responded.

"Coral is coming home with me," he announced to Ron who arrived a few minutes ago. "I already have my driver taking us home. Also, I'll need you to return her rental car. Coral, do you have your key?"

"Right here," I said, extending the key that I dug from my pocket. I had already planned to exchange the rental, figuring that whoever broke into my suit likely already spotted my rental and knew which one it was. Liam was giving out orders so quickly that I hadn't gotten a chance to tell him that. As long as it had been since we served together, it felt natural to follow Li's lead. As much as I didn't want to, I trusted Liam wholeheartedly, and he was about the only person I trusted in this situation.

"I'll have to call Jabari to let him know what's happened," I told Liam as we headed to the elevators.

"It's late, you can call him tomorrow," he returned, as the doors open.

I glanced at my phone to check the time and realized it was after ten our time, which meant it was after eleven in Savannah. I made a mental note to call Jabari in the morning and fill him in. "I'll need a car to get around."

"You can use one of mine."

I shook my head. "Liam, that's not necessary. I can get another rental."

"You'll use one of mine," he said with finality, putting his hand at the small of my back to exit the elevator.

We exited through a back entrance where there was a car already waiting for us. Liam waved the driver off, and held the door open for me. The driver stuck my suitcase in the trunk and we left. The ride was silent for the first few minutes. I stared out the window, taking in the city lights for a little while and going over in my head who could be behind the break-in. I made a plan to make a trip to the junkyard to inspect Larry's car. At this point, I was convinced there had been foul play in his accident.

"I'm going to have to speak with Jeremy about this first thing in the morning."

His admonishing tone alerted me to one fact. He was pissed.

"Liam, this wasn't Jeremy's fault," I attempted to calm him.

"Bullshit. He runs this hotel and everything in it. No one should have been able to break into any guest's room, let alone yours." He stared right at me and even in the dimly lit car I could see his lower jaw working. I inched over a little closer to him and grabbed his clenched fist, massaging it until he fully opened it and took my hand.

"I'm fine. Don't blame Jeremy for this. There are over a thousand guests in that hotel, with even more employees. You haven't had any safety issues before. It's not on him. Maybe it's..." I trailed off with the realization that whoever had been after me for some time now had possibly found me in Dallas. Maybe this wasn't about Li or his company, but about me.

I turned my head to look out the window, contemplating the issue in my head. Once again, I began to have doubts about staying with Liam at his home. I had kept my distance from my own family for fear of them getting hurt, and now my concern was turned towards Li and his family.

Liam must have sensed my hesitation because he tugged on my hand. "Hey," he whispered. "I'm not having you stay anywhere else but under my roof. And you will tell me what it is you're hiding. I can't help you if you don't tell me everything."

I snatched my hand back and moved over, putting distance between us. This little moment started to feel too intimate. What got to me the most was that I started to tell him everything. I wanted to let him in so I didn't have to carry the burden alone anymore, but I couldn't do that. It was my cross to bear. "I don't need your help, Li. I came here to do a job and then move on. Just as I've been doing for years."

He stared at me through silence, up until we arrived at his home. Out of the corner of my eye, I noticed the driver punch in a code which opened the huge iron gate. Liam's gaze was still firmly planted on me and I couldn't look away. I wasn't going to tell him what was going on with me.

"Sir," the driver called from up front.

"It's okay, Leo. I got it," Liam replied, finally turning his head to open the car door. He held it open for me, taking my hand to help me out.

I bent and retrieved my suitcase from the driver and turned towards the house for the first time. I looked up at the huge mansion in front of me. There were at least three levels, numerous huge windows, and even the doors were made of glass. Since I was unable to see directly into the home, I could only assume that they were made with a specialized glass. I noticed the stone siding around the huge door and lower portion of the house, while the rest of the siding was made up of a brownish brick. At first glance, one would liken the home to a log cabin style, but it was much too massive to fit that definition. I tilted my head to the side, took in the beauty of the home before me, and I got that feeling as if I was seeing something again. This house almost looked familiar. I knew I'd never been there, and Liam said he had it built only a couple of years ago. I had visited Li's childhood home many times and this was not it.

"Your home is beautiful," I said, noticing the awe in my own voice.

He gave me that half-smile of his. "Thank you. It's..." he trailed off, clearing his throat.

I knew he wanted to say something more, but I didn't press him. I turned back to the house and looked again before I felt Liam remove the suitcase from my hand, and place his other hand at the small of my back to guide me to the door. Once inside, he turned on the light and the entire front portion of the home illuminated. The modern style decor and light grey colored furniture gave the home a comfortable, yet classy feel.

"Laura's sleep by now. I have her nanny stay over on the nights I have to work late," he stated just above a whisper.

"Okay."

"The room you'll be staying in is on the second level next to mine," he informed me as he closed and locked the door behind us, and ushered me towards the stairs. "There's an elevator you can use to get from the first, second, third or basement levels." He pointed out the elevator once we arrive at the second level. "I usually don't use it late because it's next to Laura's room and she's a light sleeper," he said smiling. That smile did something to me and I found myself having to look away. It was still shocking to think of Liam as a dad, but I could tell he loved his daughter with everything in him. Just like a father should.

"This is your room," he said once we made our way down the hall. He turned and opened the door; inside there was a huge bed right in the middle of the room. "You have a fully-stocked private bathroom. He pointed with his thumb over his shoulder to the door behind him. "My room is right across the hall. I get up pretty early so when you awake you can head down to the kitchen. It's on the first floor, make a right from the stairs and follow the hallway down. You can't miss it. Goodnight." He stepped closer, placing his hand around my waist. I looked up in anticipation of his kiss, but instead he used his lips to gently caress my cheek as his hand squeezed my waist. I felt his warm breath on my face, causing me to slightly shiver.

"Thank you," I said as his lips were still on me.

A second later, he pulled back. "Don't thank me. This should..." he stopped himself again and ran his knuckles along my cheek before pulling back. He jerked his head towards the room and I obliged. "Go inside."

Once inside the room, I closed the door behind me and leaned back against it trying to get my bearings. I'd been trying to keep as much distance between myself and Liam for a week, and now I was staying under the same roof. I sighed as I slipped off my boots, and grabbed my tablet and laptop. I figured working was the best thing I could do right now to get my thoughts off of Liam. I needed to get to the bottom of this case and get it over with so I could move on. I reviewed the notes I'd been taking of the interviews we'd conducted, I scheduled a time for the next day to go visit the junkyard, and even with Liam's offer to use one of his cars, I still made a note to visit another rental car dealership.

After a few hours, I started to feel the weight of the day, so I headed to the shower. I took my time in the shower, noticing the numerous different types of soaps, hair products and moisturizers in the bathroom. For a split second, I wondered if Liam had this set up for other women he'd had stay over. I thought back to the look on his face as he'd stood in the doorway. My thoughts and feelings became scrambled as I remembered the tenderness in his eyes. My last thoughts as I drifted off to sleep were of the look on Liam's face before I shut the door…it was a mix of want and something else that I still couldn't quite pinpoint.

CHAPTER 10

$\mathcal{C}$*oral*

I woke up to sunlight streaming in from the huge bedroom window. As I stretched, I was surprised to find that I'd slept much later than normal, so I decided to postpone my morning workout routine. Since I was going to the junkyard today, I dressed a little more casual than normal, opting for a pair of dark blue skinny jeans, a tan sweater, and a pair of lace up sneakers.

After moisturizing and getting dressed, I fluffed my hair a little, happy to see the curly ringlets holding up well, and then grabbed my tablet and phone to head downstairs. I remembered the direction Liam told me to go towards the kitchen. Just outside the entrance I heard movement, and I stopped, rethinking whether or not I should go in, or try to quietly slip out before anyone noticed me. Unfortunately, my grumbling stomach had other ideas. It wouldn't have hurt to eat before I left.

I continued to the huge kitchen and the first person I saw was Laura sitting at the table, singing her ABC's and dancing a little as she ate cut up blueberry pancakes off her plate. She stopped suddenly, turned, and looked right at me. I was struck by her resemblance to Liam. He couldn't deny this little girl even if he wanted to. Her green

"

eyes widened slightly, before crinkling a little as her mouth broke into a big smile.

"Hi," she said cheerily, and waving.

My heart strings tugged and I couldn't help but be drawn to her. "Good morning, Princess," I smiled and waved back to her.

Her eyes got really wide with cheer. "My daddy calls me that!"

I raised my eyebrows. I didn't know Li called her that. I'd just said it because it came naturally.

"He does?" I asked as I make my way closer, stooping down in front of her.

She nodded with excitement. "Yup! He says that all little girls should be treated like princesses," she giggled. It was one of the best sounds I'd heard in a long time.

"Your daddy is a very smart man," I told her, pinching the bridge of her nose, which caused her to giggle even more. The sound was infectious and before I knew it, I had joined in on the laughter.

"What are you eating?" I asked, looking over at her plate.

"Pancakes." She held out her little pink colored plastic fork showing me a piece of her cut up breakfast.

"Well, I'll be!" I heard a familiar voice behind me and stood.

My lips spread into a grin. "Hello, Ms. Mary."

"Coral Coleman. Girl, if you don't get over here and give me a hug."

Ms. Mary was Liam's long-term nanny and then housekeeper in his childhood home. I hadn't seen her in years. I moved to embrace her and she squeezed me tighter than I had been hugged in years. It reminded me of the way my mother used to hug me after she'd gotten sick. As if she'd known her time with me had been precious. I hated thinking about that, so I pulled away and looked down at Ms. Mary's dark chocolate colored skin. She was well into her sixties, but could pass for much younger. She was probably a good size sixteen but carried it well, and I could tell she still maintained her bi-weekly hair appointments because there was not a grey hair to be found in her relaxed hair as it rested on her shoulders.

"How are you?" I asked, looking down at her.

"Oh, I'm just fine," she waved her hands, "Just cleaning up after this little Missy," she said as she ruffled the hair on Laura's head, causing another fit of giggles.

"So, I see Li still had you doing his dirty work," I teased.

"Tuh, you know that boy can't get rid of me. Truth is, he tried. Gave me a nice severance and everything after Laurence and I married."

That wasn't much of a surprise. Laurence was Liam's father's landscaper. I knew they'd had a thing for one another.

"But I still wanted to do something part time now that Laurence opened his own company with his two boys. I'm only here in the mornings and it keeps me busy. You know an old woman has to keep herself occupied." She laughed.

"I wouldn't know. I don't see any old women around here."

"Oh, Coral. You're still as sweet as punch."

I chuckled at that. There weren't not many people in this world who would call me sweet.

Ms. Mary gestured towards Laura. "I see you've met Missy here,"

"Yes, I have."

"My daddy said a friend needed help and is staying with us. Is that you?" Laura asked.

I knelt back down in front of her. "You're one smart kid," I said, proud of the way she put two and two together. "Yes, I'm your daddy's friend and I am staying here for a little bit. Is that okay with you?" I asked. Honestly, if she were to have any strange feelings about it, I would have had no problem packing up and leaving. I didn't want to make anything uncomfortable for Li or his daughter.

She shook her head emphatically. "No. I think you're funny and I like your hair." She reached out and rubbed her hand on one of my auburn colored curls.

"Thank you. I like your hair too," I said, fingering a few of her blond locks.

"Good morning," Liam's voice chimed in breaking up the sweet little moment between Laura and myself, causing me to wonder if he witnessed the interaction between us.

I stood and turned to see a shirtless Liam in a pair of basketball shorts and sneakers. The air immediately rushed from my body. It was obvious that he'd just finished working out because his bronzed skin was covered in a sheen of sweat. I eyed the tattoo on his chest and the scar on his abdomen that still made my heart rate speed up. My eyes traveled up his pectoral muscles to his strong jaw and then his eyes, only to find that he was staring at me. His look was so intense I felt as if he was reaching out and touching me.

"Daddy!" Laura yelled. She hopped down from her chair to run into her father's awaiting arms, where he swooped her up and planted a kiss on her cheeks.

"Good morning, Princess. Did you finish breakfast?"

"Yes. Daddy, today we're going to the zoo and then to the library."

"You are? Now, that sounds like fun."

I unconsciously smiled at the interaction between Liam and Laura. His smile grew and my heart did that stupid flip flopping thing again as I watched them.

Just then, the doorbell rang.

"There's Anna now," Liam told Laura.

"Yay!" she clapped.

"Come on, Little Missy," Ms. Mary called out.

"Okay, Princess. Have fun and don't bite the animals." He kissed the top of her head.

Laura laughed as he put her down. "Daddy, I don't bite!"

Ms. Mary grabbed her hand and exited the kitchen just as Li turned back to stare at me.

"She's beautiful, Li."

His smile widened. "She's the best part of me." His voice was filled with such emotion I knew it was the truth.

I cleared my throat, trying to move on from the moment. "Anyway, I'll be stopping at the junkyard today where Larry's car is, then I'll go back to Bennett Industries to do a few more interviews, and then I need to speak with Jabari to get his help on the laptop and let him know I'm no longer at the hotel."

He stared at me as he cocked his head to the side. I willed myself not to let my eyes drop down and stare at his washboard abs again. I almost managed it, but I was too tempted. The tattoo, the scar all reminded me of our history together. A history that was so entwined sometimes I didn't know where I stopped and Liam began. Soon I felt something cold and hard pressed against my back. I came back to my senses and realized my back was pressing against the white granite countertops. I looked up to see Liam's face only a few inches away from mine and his arms braced the edge of the counter on either side of me, effectively trapping me. That dark emerald color in his eyes had returned. I opened and closed my mouth a few times trying to form words.

"Wh-what are you doing?" I asked, trying to sound normal.

"I noticed you staring. See something you like?" The deep, richness of his voice rolled over me and I almost let out a dreamy sigh. Instead, I bit the inside of my cheek and did my best to rein my emotions in.

"Liam, stop the bullshit and go shower. You're getting your nasty sweat all over me." My words were a lie. He knew it and I knew it. Li's sweat was anything but nasty, but I was not giving in again. We'd already gone too far.

"Hmmhm."

I turned my head to the left seeing Ms. Mary had returned. From the smirk on her face, I assumed she'd watched our entire exchange. Years ago, she'd said how perfect Liam and I were for each other…no matter how much we'd insisted we were just friends. I could tell this little scene was only reigniting that same dream fairytale in her mind. It was time to extinguish those thoughts before they got too out of control.

Without turning to look back at Liam, I used my hip to bump his arm catching him off guard, and stepped out of his hold.

"Go take a shower. I need to go get a car from the rental place to use," I said, trying to change the subject and forgetting all about breakfast.

He lifted his brows and smirked. "Care to join me?"

Before I could respond, I heard Ms. Mary's laughter from behind me. "Some things never change," she said as she finished putting the last of the pots from breakfast away. "I'm heading out now. My man is taking me out to lunch and I want to make sure I look good for him. You crazy kids enjoy yourselves. I'll be back tomorrow morning." She whisked out of the room, giving us one last look and laughing again.

As I stared behind Ms. Mary, Liam said, "She always said you'd be a hard nut to crack but to be patient."

"What?" I asked, confused.

"Nothing. I'm going to shower and then we'll go to my garage to see what car will best fit your needs."

"Li—" My protest was cut off as Liam's lips met mine. The kiss was brief, a parting kiss before he turned and made his way down the hall and up the stairs to shower.

"There's green tea in the cabinets. I asked Ms. Mary to buy some this morning," he called over his shoulder.

I was left standing there trying to figure out what the heck had just happened in the last fifteen minutes. I rummaged through the cabinets, found the tea, and made some before calling Jabari. Better speaking with Jabari about this case than going over this warped relationship between Li and I.

CHAPTER 11

*L*iam

"I'm fine Jabari. It's no big deal."

I heard Coral's voice as I entered the living room area and the smile that touched my lips was instant. I was going to be one hundred percent honest right now; I was thrilled to have Coral under my roof. I dreamt of it for years. Hell, I worked for it for years. This house wasn't built on a whim.

"I told you I was fine. Let's move on to something that matters."

I frowned hearing those words. I heard Jabari's sigh of concern through the speaker phone, and knew he was probably just as concerned about Coral's safety as I was. I hated that because Coral didn't seem as worried about her own safety as she should be. My girl was tough as hell and often thought of her own safety last and went out of her way to protect those around her. Speaking of which, I knew there was something she was hiding from me. And whatever it was, it felt big. I was not about to stand by and let anything happen to her.

"Are you sure you're alright? No one was there when you entered the suite?"

"No one would have gotten within five feet of her," I answered

Jabari who had just asked that last question into Coral's speaker phone.

She abruptly turned to me and narrowed her eyes.

"Liam?" Jabari's confused voice came through the phone.

"It's me."

"How's it going? Coral tells me you found the laptop."

"Yeah, we got it, but need help getting into it.

"I can help with that. Is Coral giving you any trouble?"

I chuckled at that. "Hell yeah she is, but it's the kind of trouble I like," I said winking at Coral. She narrowed her eyes even more at me and it made me smile. I knew that look had intimidated many of her opponents, but I couldn't help think how cute she looked. All scary like that and shit. It turned me on. I know. I know. Something was wrong with me.

"*Anyway*," she stated, rolling her eyes. "My job is to make sure *you* stay out of trouble." Coral finished, glaring at me.

My smile widened as I stepped closer. "Oh? Keeping me out of trouble?" I came to stand directly in front of her, peering down into her upturned face. "But it's so much more fun when we get in trouble...together." My voice was low and deep, the innuendo in it not missed by anyone. I knew this because aside from the way Coral bit her lower lip and swallowed deeply, I also heard the chuckles ringing through the phone from Jabari.

"I see you're still the only one who can make this one speechless." Jabari continued to laugh.

"Fuck you, Bri. No one asked you," Coral chimed in only making Jabari laugh harder.

"See? Her response to me was immediate."

"Glad you all can get a laugh in at my expense. Now, can we get back to the matter at hand?" Coral pivoted and stepped around me, putting more distance between us. I listened and watched her as she continued to talk to Jabari about the case.

As she talked, I remembered that she'd be going the junkyard where Larry's totaled car still was. I had Larry's fiancé request that the vehicle not be touched until I gave the okay. I told her that he may have had some work files in there. No need informing her that her fiancé's death may have been more than just a simple accident.

I pulled out my phone to text Ron to send over Mitch, one of our top security guys. I wanted Mitch to go with Coral to the junkyard and be her tail for the remainder of this case. My gut told me Coral could use the extra security detail and after last night, I was not about to ignore my instincts.

"Alright," I began as I slid my cell back in my pocket and noticed Coral was off the phone. "Let's go see what you're driving today." I placed my hand on her lower back and began escorting her out the back entrance to my huge garage.

"I should have known." I noted the humor in her voice as she stared, shaking her head, looking at the lineup of vehicles. I only kept about five of my cars on this property. I had a storage facility for the rest.

"I bet this is only half of what you own."

I grinned and looked down at her. Those hazel eyes shining with laughter assaulted me and for a brief second, I felt as if I was falling into them. Coral must have noticed because she soon took a step away from me, breaking our physical contact and stare.

"You were close. This is about one-third of all my cars." I had been fascinated by cars since I was a kid. My home garage housed my BMW, Porsche, Lamborghini, and two Maseratis. The other ten vehicles I owned were kept in the storage facility.

"What do you need with so many cars?" she asked.

"You know better than that, CeCe. It's not because I need them. It's my appreciation of them. I'm a collector."

"Whatever. These are all way too pricey for me to drive around town for however long I'm here."

The reminder that she was only here for as long as this case was open was a punch to the gut. If I'd had it my way, she'd already know her stay here was anything but temporary.

"Nonsense," I said. "How about the Beamer? You should be familiar with driving one. You still have it?" I asked, changing topic a bit.

She turned, looked directly at me, and I knew she knew exactly what I was referring to. As a graduation present, I had given Coral a brand new BMW. It was a beautiful white with cream colored leather seats. I searched for weeks thinking of what to get her for graduation and as soon as I saw it, I pictured her in the front seat. In my mind, her mocha colored skin paired with the white and cream colors looked perfect. Of course, my father was pissed when he found out, but ask me if I gave a shit what he thought. The look of surprise, awe, and joy on her face had been gift enough for me. Though, after those emotions, came the guilt. She felt ashamed at having purchased a pair of monogrammed cufflinks and a matching monogrammed briefcase for me, but those gifts had been perfect. She knew one day after my military career I'd take the helm at Bennett Industries and wanted me to be prepared. I wore the cufflinks almost every day, and I used the briefcase so much it got beat up and I had to get a new one. I still have it though. Those were the little ways I kept her close to me when she wasn't physically near.

"Yes. I still have it," she finally responded.

I smiled internally knowing she kept my gift as well.

"I bet it has less than one-hundred thousand miles on it," I retorted.

She smiled and shrugged. "What can I say? I spent four of my seven years of my military career in the desert and since you..." she paused "...since getting out of the Army, I've spent a lot of time over-seas. Plus, I bought my own car. I have an Audi."

I raised my eyebrows, impressed. "I taught you well."

"You wish," she waved me off and turned towards the shiny black BMW. "Are you sure you don't mind me using one of your cars? I can just get another rent—"

I held my hand up, cutting her off. "Why would you want some rental? God knows how many asses have sat in the driver seat. Why not just take my barely used baby right here?" I pulled the key out of my pocket. I had a feeling she would choose the Beamer. I felt safer with her driving one of my cars because I knew none of these had been touched by anyone but me, and all my cars were equipped with gps tracking that went directly to my phone. I left out that last part though.

"Alright. I'll use the BMW. I'll be here for another two to three weeks tops, anyway, and I don't think I'll be driving too much," she shrugged.

That tightness in my chest began to build at the mention of her leaving. My phone vibrated in my pocket, interrupting my thoughts. I pulled it out and nodded at the message I just received.

"Great, and it looks like Mitch has just arrived to go with you to the junkyard."

She crinkled her brows at me. "Why would Mitch go with me to the junkyard?" Her voice was laced with a hint of warning and irritation.

"Because someone broke into your hotel suite last night and until we figure out who, Mitch will be escorting you wherever you go if I'm not with you," I answered honestly. Did I know Coral could take care of herself? Yes. Should she have had to? No. That's why Mitch was here.

"Did you forget who the security specialist is here?" she asked, hands on her hips, head cocked to the side, eyeballing me.

"Sweetheart, I haven't forgotten anything. I also haven't forgotten the feeling of my heart pulsating with terror at the thought of anything happening to you."

Her eyes widened and I could tell she wasn't expecting that.

"I don't need an escort."

"You'll have one anyway," I insisted. "My woman is not going around town investigating murders and corporate cover ups without someone watching her back at all times." I damn near growled the last part.

"I'm not yours," she retorted.

That declaration pissed me off. In two quick steps I was in front of her and wrapped my arms around her waist. "You've been mine since we were eighteen years old!" I actually growled that time before taking her lips in a possessive kiss. I used my tongue to outline her lips before diving in fully and taking possession of her mouth. She tried to resist at first, but soon gave in and kissed me with just as much emotion. Her body knew where it belonged, even if she refused to accept it.

"See, even your body knows," I gloated once I pulled back. We were both panting heavily and I could feel my erection beginning to strain against my pants. I didn't mind being a little late for work...

"Mr. Bennett." That thought was interrupted when Mitch called out from behind me. I told the security gate to let him in, a decision I now regretted.

Coral quickly stepped back, snatching the key from my hand and going over to the car. "Mitch, we'll be heading over to the Morrison junkyard. Do you know where that is?" she asked, doing her best to avoid looking at me. I knew she was not as unaffected as she appeared to be. I could make out the outline of her nipples protruding through her sweater.

"Stubborn woman," I mumbled. "Make sure you keep a close eye on her," I warned Mitch, pausing to make full eye contact. "There are two people I care about most in this world—my daughter and that headstrong woman over there," I motioned towards Coral. "She's tougher than you and smarter. She may try to lose you, but it's your ass if anything happens to her." I looked him straight in the eye so he knew I was not bullshitting. I could tell he was a little shocked by the underlying threat in my tone, but he needed to know I meant every word of what I said.

He nodded. "Yes sir, Mr. Bennett. Her safety is of the utmost importance."

"Good." I turned to see Coral now in the driver's seat. I moved to the wall and pressed the button to raise the garage door. As it rose, I strolled over to the car and tapped the passenger side window. "I'll see you in my office around one for lunch. One o'clock," I said with finality when I saw she was going to object.

She rolled her eyes as she mumbled, "Whatever."

I stepped back in time to get out of her way as she pulled off, exiting the garage.

"You better catch up," I said, turning to Mitch.

He hurriedly exited the garage to get to his own vehicle and follow Coral. I pulled out my phone and activated the gps tracker.

"I can't wait until this shit is over," I said to myself, thinking about the first meeting I had scheduled.

CHAPTER 12

oral

"Ouch!" I squealed as Mitch stepped on the back of my heel, yet again. He was sticking to me like white on rice and I had no doubt it was because Li told him to. I looked over my shoulder and saw the worried look in Mitch's eyes, and I knew Li probably even threatened him. At six feet, with a bulky muscular build of his own, one wouldn't think Mitch would be intimidated by many, but then again, you hadn't seen Liam's threatening glare. I'd seen more men than I could count cower in the face of it.

"You know, Mitch, you don't have to be so close. I'm not trying to make a break for it or anything." I glanced at him over my shoulder again as we continued to walk down the row of damaged and battered vehicles. Mitch took the hint, and he gave me a little more breathing room. I sighed as I still saw him out of the corner of my eye. I couldn't believe Liam had actually assigned me a damn body guard. Then again, that was a lie. I could believe it. He'd always been protective; even though he was very much aware I could handle myself.

I stopped as we approached a dark blue 2014 Lexus. I pulled my cell out my pocket to pull up an image of Larry's car and matched the license plate number.

106

"X21..." I mumbled, reading off the license number. Sure enough, it was a match. Of course, the wreckage in front of me was nothing like the car in the picture. It was obvious the car was in a horrific accident and there was no way anyone in the driver's seat could have survived. I made my way around the mangled vehicle, pulling out my Nikon to snap pictures from every angle before touching it. I made my way to the front of the car to lift the hood.

"Hey Mitch, can you see if you can reach in and pull the lever to release the hood?"

"Sure thing." He moved to reach through where the door used to be of the driver's seat. The door had to be removed by the Jaws of Life to cut Larry out. By the time rescuers got to him, it was too late. Thinking about Larry took me back to my own mission. I remembered my team members who'd never made it home to their loved ones because someone had been after me. I clenched my fists thinking that whoever killed my teammates might also be behind Larry's death. Whoever this bastard was, he needed to be stopped.

"How's that?" Mitch's voice interrupted my thoughts.

I moved to raise the hood and after a few hard pulls I was able to lift it. "Got it. Thanks," I told him. Looking over the contents of the hood, I did a quick scan of the different parts; aside from the mess of the wreckage nothing looked out of place. Thinking back to police pictures of the scene, I recalled not seeing any skid marks, which was highly suspect in an accident. I reached my hand down to feel for the brake line. I ran my hand along it and sure enough, just as I suspected, there was a tear. I snapped a quick picture before closing the hood.

I moved to the passenger side of the car where the door was dented. Mitch helped me pull it open and I managed to squeeze inside, looking around for anything out of the ordinary. I looked over at the driver's seat where Larry's dried blood still stained the leather. I'd dealt with enough gory scenes in my life that the sight of blood did nothing to me.

Reaching under the dashboard, I felt around before opening the dashboard's compartment and found it emptied. However, I got the nagging feeling there was something inside. Larry's accident supposedly occurred after nine at night while he was on his way home from work. A few days prior, he'd scheduled a meeting with Liam and Jeremy about the company's books. That couldn't have been a coincidence.

Just as I had this thought, my fingers ran along the underside of the driver's seat. I felt something. Gripping it, I could tell it'd been stuck to the seat with duct tape. Pulling it off, I saw it was a flash drive.

"Bingo!" I whispered excitedly. I knew this flash drive held whatever Larry wanted Li and Jeremy to know. "Mitch!" I called out, exiting the vehicle and closing the door. "We're done here. We can tell the junkyard owner he can now destroy the car." I left the junkyard with the feeling we'd just reached a major break in the case.

* * *

"Ms. Coleman, Mr. Bennett has been expecting you," Li's assistant informed me as soon as I entered through the office glass doors. "He said to tell you to go on in as soon as you entered." I knew by the way she was rushing me, Li had probably been asking her every five minutes if I'd arrived.

"Thank you," I told her as I walked past her desk to Li's door. I knocked a couple times before entering.

Li glanced up at me as I walked in. "Yeah Richard, I hear you," he said.

I listened intently, realizing that Li was talking to his father. He and his father never really got along. Richard Bennett was always more worried about power and money than the actual well-being of his son. As soon as I met Liam's father, I knew he didn't care too much for me. Didn't bother me because the feeling was mutual.

"Listen Richard, we'll talk more when I'm in Austin later this week. I have to go." He hung up abruptly.

I raised my eyebrows at this news. I had no idea Liam was going to Austin. "How is the governor these days?" I asked, closing his office door behind me.

Li snorted derisively. "Still breathing," he mumbled to himself so low I barely caught the words. "You're late." He glared at me accusingly, changing the subject.

I shrugged. "It's not like you didn't know where I was. I'm sure your trusty gps told you the BMW had been parked in the garage for the last forty-five minutes." I smirked as I strolled over to his desk and plopped down in the chair across from him.

Li grinned and sat back in his chair, folding his hands behind his head.

"Didn't think I'd realize you were tracking my every move?"

"No, I knew you'd figure it out eventually. I just wanted to see how long it'd take," he said, giving me that cocky grin of his. It was funny how different his demeanor was now than less than five minutes ago when he was on the phone with his father.

"Took me all of five minutes. Of course, I would have realized sooner if I hadn't been distracted by other...things," I admitted thinking of that kiss he planted on my lips right before I got in the car.

"Oh yeah? Like what?" he leaned in.

"You don't need your ego stroked anymore. Anyway," I said standing and relocating to the couch in the office. "I'm hungry. Feed me so we can get on with other matters."

"You wouldn't be so hungry if you had brought your ass here at one o'clock like I said," he admonished as he stood from behind his desk. "It'd serve you right if I'd already eaten and left you to fend for yourself," he frowned down at me.

Damn, I love that face.

Whoa! Where the hell did that come from?

"Whatever, Li. We both know what happens when I get too hungry so there's no way you'd leave me hanging. Where's the food?" I said to distract myself from my previous thoughts. We both knew I turned into your worst enemy when I hadn't eaten in a while. I'd been known to go off on someone more than once when hungry.

Li walked backed to his desk and pressed the speaker on his office phone. "Darla, can you send our lunch in please? Thank you."

A few minutes later, we sat across from one another munching on chicken salad sandwiches and kettle chips.

"What did you find?" Liam asked as he sipped from his bottle of water.

"How do you know I found anything?"

The bottle paused halfway to his mouth and he gave me a "don't play with me" look, which of course caused me to smirk.

"You spent a few hours at the accident sate and the junkyard, and then you were here for at least forty-five minutes before you came up to my office. I know you found something."

"Damn GPS," I muttered. "Well, for one, I'm one-hundred percent convinced we're dealing with a murder. This was no accident."

Liam lifted an eyebrow at me. "Tell me," he insisted, sitting forward in his chair, leaning in closer to me.

"It was raining hard the night of Larry's accident. I checked the weather records and the police report. They put down the freezing rain as the cause of the accident. But, the lack of skid marks on the road led me to believe one of two things."

"Either he was incapacitated at the time of the accident or someone fucked with his brakes," Li stated, interrupting me.

I cocked my head to the side, eyeing him. "Can you not interrupt me?"

He grinned. "I'm sorry, CeCe. Continue."

"Thank you. Anyway, I went to the junkyard and checked out the car. Took pictures, checked under the hood, and felt the brake line and sure enough—"

He nodded knowingly. "It was cut."

"Yup. Someone wanted Larry dead and…" I reached in my pocket and tossed the flash drive into Liam's hands. "I'm betting whatever's on here is the reason."

"Where'd you find this?" he asked, staring at the drive.

"Taped underneath the driver seat. If Larry was as smart as I believed he was, we may not even need to get into his laptop. Everything we need may be on the drive."

His tone was a little surprised. "You haven't checked it out yet?"

I shook my head. "Not yet. When I went to the junkyard, the owner told me a man had stopped by a couple days ago to see Larry's car. When he refused him, he said the man became agitated. But the owner was under strict instructions from your office to not let anyone who wasn't cleared first to see the vehicle."

"Did he give you a description of this guy?"

I nodded as I took another sip of my water. "Said he was around five-ten, stocky, looked Hispanic."

Li paused and looked me right in the eye. I knew this was coming.

"Yeah, so I came back here and had Ron do a "follow up" interview with Rodrigo," I said, using air quotes around follow up. Rodrigo was one of the building's night time security guards. The description the owner of the junkyard gave immediately brought Rodrigo to mind. So, I had Ron do another interview to ask Rodrigo if he saw Larry the night of his death. I made sure not to mention anything about what I found at the junkyard.

"And what's your read on him?" Li asked.

"He knows something. His guilt was plain as day. I'm just not sure how much he knows."

"Motherfuck!" Li cursed, slamming his water bottle down on the table.

"Li," I said in my calming voice.

"No, fuck that, CeCe. These bastards work for me. These are supposed to be my people. We're supposed to be doing some good here. Who the fuck is behind this?" He looked me straight in the eye.

"I don't know, but we're going to find out." I insisted.

"No!"

"No? What do you mean no?"

"I mean, this shit has gone too far. They killed Larry. Broke into your hotel suite. Now you're going around half-cocked investigating all by yourself. No. You're putting yourself in harm's way." He stood seething as he paced.

I paused, squinting as I look at him. "Li," I called. The muscles in his jaw flexed as he refused to look at me. "Liam," I called more sternly, the second time, standing.

Finally, he turned to look at me.

"Where the hell do you think I've been the last five years? Out to lunch? Relaxing on the beach of some exotic island?" My voice became louder.

"CeCe."

"No," I held my hand up stopping him. "I've dealt with killers, war criminals, terrorists, for more than a decade of my life. Even after leaving the agency. I don't need you getting in your feelings about safety. I know what the hell I'm doing which is why Jeremy called me in the first place."

"Dammit, Coral. I know better than anyone how capable you are of getting this done."

"Then what the hell are you talking about?" I demanded, placing my hands on my hips.

"I'm talking about keeping *you* safe. I'm talking about the fact that I don't know if I could breathe if something were to happen to you. As close as I am to..." he paused, running his hand through his thick hair.

"To what?"

"Nothing. Just know *nothing* is going to happen to you. I won't let it."

"Liam, we're not talking about me. This is about your company. Someone killed your employee. The same person may be trying to steal money or secrets or something from your business."

"But someone is targeting you, aren't they? Someone connected to this case?"

I stood, stunned. I wondered how he had put it together. I never told anyone about Ghost or whoever it was that apparently wanted me dead.

"You're not the only one who can read others. I know you. I could tell you were holding something back from the start of this case."

"I don't know what you're talking about." I tried to deflect, but should have known better.

In two long strides, Liam was right in my face. "So, this is how you want to play it? You're going to pretend like I'm making shit up? Fine.

You'll keep working to find out who is doing this but now you'll have two bodyguards on you at all times."

"Have you lost your damn mind? I've been doing this too long to be followed by some incompetent bodyguards. Besides, it looks like most of the damn problems are coming from your security staff anyway. How do we know the leak about my hotel suite didn't come from one of them? How do you know any of them can be trusted?"

For the first time since this conversation began, Liam's face relaxed into his usual arrogant expression. "Already thought of, Sweetheart. I've personally vetted Mitch, which was why he was with you earlier today, and Brian agreed to take a short leave from his position to act as temporary bodyguard."

"You can't be se—"

"Hey Bennett," Brian interrupted as he entered Liam's office.

The frown on my face deepened as the men exchanged greetings. I stood akimbo, glaring at both of them. "Brian, I don't know what this..." I paused pointing at Li, "asshole told you, but there is no need for you to follow me around like some lost damn puppy."

Brian began laughing, which only spiked my anger.

"The hell is so damn funny?" I demanded.

"I told you she'd be livid about this."

I turned as another familiar deep voice entered the conversation. Jeremy came strolling in the office.

"You're goddamn right I'm livid. Didn't you bring me here to find out what was going on? Why am I being treated like the damn case instead of the security consultant you hired?!" My voice rose with anger as I pointed at Jeremy. I couldn't even look at Liam who I knew was responsible for all of this.

"Coral, I know you don't want this, but it was the only way that he," Jeremy motioned to Liam, "would agree to keep you on this case and not locked up in his house. I've already fired the head of my hotel's security for that shit in your suite, and if I didn't have to travel so much for work, I would be the one on your detail, but I can't."

I stared into Jeremy's forest green eyes and saw he meant every word. He looked like he belonged on the pages of a GQ Magazine bad boy issue with his long dark hair pulled into a low ponytail, and the neck tattoo peeking out from under his collar. But I also knew Jeremy was as deadly as anyone in this room. I looked around at all three of the stern faces in the office. Of course, Liam's was the sternest of them all; although each one of their faces the same thing—they were not letting this go.

"I'm not letting this drop so you might as well forget it." His tone was rigid.

"Whatever," I said like some petulant teenager who hadn't gotten their way. I stormed out of Liam's office with Brian right behind me as we headed toward the elevator. "I'm going to look through a few more of these interviews and then I'm going for a run," I told Brian over my shoulder as we entered the open elevator doors.

"Liam already told me you like to go for a run to blow off steam, so my gym bag is packed and in the car."

I raised an eyebrow curiously.

"What you think I can't keep up?" he asked, jokingly.

"I don't know," I responded with a shrug. "Maybe civilian life had made you soft." I teased.

"Or my injury?"

At that, I shrugged again.

He lifted his right pants leg a few inches and I saw the titanium and aluminum metals that were now a substitute for his missing leg. "Lightweight and fits like a glove. Don't worry about my ability to keep up. I run up to seventy miles a week and I missed my run this morning," he winked and lowered his pant leg.

I smiled at that. "Good. Let's go," I called over my shoulder as we exited the elevator.

CHAPTER 13

Liam

I knew assigning bodyguards to Coral would tick her off. It'd been a week and she was still barely speaking to me. The only time she said more than two words to me was at night when we were home with Laura. Those two had practically been stuck at the hip every night for the last week. Hell, Laura even asked Coral to read her bedtime stories at night instead of me. When Coral realized Laura's bedtime story was actually Tasha's latest book, I could see the expression on her face soften. Ever since, they spent at least a half an hour reading to one another about a little girl saving the planet from foreign and alien invaders. I would be jealous; but I was secretly terrified of how these two would get along. I should have known better. I mean, not only was Coral a natural caretaker, she had always had a special affinity for kids. I even saw it in Iraq when she once intervened in a domestic dispute when a local father attempted to beat his young daughter. Our whole squad was horrified at the scene, but Coral was on her feet and in the guy's face before we could blink. From then on, while we remained stationed there, she did her best to check in on the little girl.

It was Friday and Laura was going over her grandparents' house for the weekend. Michele's parents made it a point to take Laura every other weekend. They were good people and I still hurt for them over the loss of their daughter.

"Okay, promise you'll wait until I get back to read," Laura demanded of Coral.

"Cross my heart and hope to die, stick a needle in my eye," Coral said, making a cross over her heart with her hand. She held up three fingers as if she's really pledging. This caused Laura to giggle.

"Alright, Princess, I think grandma and grandpa are outside waiting for you," I interrupted, scooping Laura in my arms.

"Yay!" Laura yelled as I carried her and her bags out of the room. "Bye!" she gave a final wave to Coral.

"See ya later, Princess," Coral called and my chest tightened at the natural bond they seemed to have established.

"It's really great that Michele's parents spend so much time with her," Coral said a few minutes later, once everyone had left.

Besides the security I had around the clock, it was just us two at the house. I was scheduled to leave for Austin in the morning. But before leaving I was determined to break this little ice that had developed between us. I'd already decided I was not letting this woman walk away from me after the case was over. I'd spent too many years without her. I wouldn't make that same mistake twice. It was time to make my play for my Queen.

"Want to play a game of chess?"

"What?" Her eyes widened as she looked at me, surprised.

"Chess? You know the board game with a sixty-four square board and sixteen pieces?"

"Haha. Very funny," she retorted, giving me a deadpan expression.

"Come on, it's not like you were doing anything anyway, besides going up to your room to try and ignore me for the rest of the night."

She rolled her eyes. "Whatever, Li. Sure, let's play."

"I have a board set up in my game room," I explained, placing my hand at the small of her back and guiding her down the hall to the huge den I referred to as my game room. In addition to my chessboard, I also had a huge flat screen with a gaming console, foosball table, and air hockey table. It was the only room in the house Laura wasn't allowed to play in. This was daddy's kingdom. I pulled out the chessboard that had the pieces already arranged. I turned to look over my shoulder to see Coral staring at a picture on the wall.

"Why do you have this here?" Her voice was low, contemplative.

I had a number of pictures hanging on the wall from my military days. Many were with the guys in our squad. Brian and Ron were even in a couple. But the biggest picture was of me and Coral. It was a picture from Afghanistan. We were just goofing around, playing a game of pickup basketball on base. Out of nowhere, Coral jumped on my back to try and get the ball and I started cracking up. Someone in our brigade snapped the picture and later gave it to me.

"It's one of my favorites of us." I ran my finger along the backside of her arm as she stood with her back to me still facing the picture.

She sighed heavily and lowered her head. "I don't get you," she nearly whispered. "I thought I knew everything about you, but I don't." Her voice trailed off.

"You do," I said fiercely. I gripped her by the arms and spun her around so she was facing me. "You know me better than anyone in this world."

She shook her head cutting me off. "Don't." She stepped back. "Let's just play chess." She moved around me and went to sit at the table where I'd set up the game.

I lowered my head in defeat. I wanted to tell her so much, but I just couldn't right now. I moved to the table to sit. Per tradition, Coral made the first move as we prepared to play. I smiled at the memory of the first time we played.

"Remember the first time I taught you chess?" I questioned as I moved my first pawn.

Her lips curled into a nostalgic smile. "I had no idea what I was doing."

"But you were a fast learner, as always."

We continued to reminisce. We talked about all types of memories from college and beyond. I remembered back to the night that I made the decision to officially join the military. Although I was in ROTC, I still had until the end of my sophomore year to decide whether or not I wanted to continue through the rest of my college career, which meant I would join the Army after graduating. At first, I just thought I'd do the first two years and leave it at that. But after meeting Coral and learning she had no choice but to join if she wanted to keep her scholarship, it made me consider signing on more seriously. By the end of our second year in college, we were already well into war in Afghanistan and war in Iraq was inevitable. I knew Coral would be heading there soon after we graduated and I wanted to be right by her side. It wasn't the burning desire to fight for my country that made me sign up. It was instinctive, to protect this woman. It's the same reason I left her side five years ago.

Her soft voice broke into my thoughts. "What are you thinking about?"

"You." I didn't hesitate answering her question. "How are Stacey and Tasha?" I asked, changing the subject.

A look of pride overcame her face and she sat back in her chair. "They're really good. Stace is married to—"

"Andre Collins," I answered.

Tilting her head to the side and staring at me she asked, "How'd you know?"

"The same way I know Tasha is living in Vermont and working on book number four. I had people watching them over the years."

Her eyes widened as she sat up in her chair. "Why would you do that?"

At that point I could've made something up or go with the truth. *Fuck it.*

"I told you I looked for you for the last five years. When I couldn't find a trace of you on your own, I knew the two people you'd never not keep in contact with were Stacey and Tasha."

"And what'd you find?"

I let out a huff. "Nothing at first, but then about a year after you disappeared and Stacey relocated to Atlanta, one of my guys caught a glimpse of you before you left again. I didn't do any serious tapping, I just kept track of them to be in the know in case anything happened to you and especially to look after Tasha. I know she hasn't met the rest of your family still."

Coral simply stared at me for a long time. I knew she's trying to figure something out. Trying to figure out why someone who left her the way I did would go through such lengths to then keep tabs on her.

"Then why..." her question was cut off by her ringing phone. She stood to retrieve it from the other side of the room.

I tracked her movements and saw her look at the caller and hit ignore. My mouth turned downward into a frown. Given that it was a Friday night, I knew it was most likely not anything work-related or else she would have answered it. I also knew it probably wasn't Stacey or Tasha because she would have answered those calls immediately. Over the past week, I'd seen her do this a couple of times when she didn't think I was paying attention. Other times, I'd seen her smile a little too wide as she exchanged text messages. My gut told me who was on the other end of those messages and the thought had my fingers itching to hit something.

"Tell Nathaniel I said hello," I called over to her. I knew it was petty, but oh well. The thought of him holding any of her attention brought out my jealousy.

"What are you king about?" she said, placing her phone back on the table and sitting on the couch. "Let's watch a movie."

I decided to go along with her little deflection for now. "How about the latest X-Men movie." I suggested knowing she appreciated action films as much as I did.

"Sounds good to me."

I turned on the TV and pulled up the movie as I slid into the seat next to her. Without giving it a second thought, I pulled Coral into my side as the opening credits started, and to my satisfaction, she didn't resist. We spent the next two hours in that position, her head leaning on my chest, my arm wrapped around her shoulder. I swear this woman was made just for me. She fit me perfectly. I began stroking her arm as the end credits rolled.

"It's been so long since I've sat and watched a movie," she sighed.

"Same here. Well, any movie that's not animated that involves a talking fish or other animal." We both laughed.

"Laura's a real character. I bet she keeps you on your toes," she sat up and smiled at me.

I groaned. "You don't know the half of it."

"She loves you. You're a good dad." Her voice was full of reverence that I felt unworthy of. She made a face that I couldn't quite read and looked down at her hands.

In that moment she appeared so vulnerable.

So innocent and soft.

I had to touch her.

I pulled her face down crushing her lips to mine. I probed her lips to open with my tongue. When they parted, I wasted little time savoring her unique taste. I rose up, pushing her down onto her back so I could climb on top of her. Her hands wrapped around my shoulders, pulling me in closer. My erection started to grow painful against the crotch of my jeans. I moved from her mouth and trailed kisses along her jawline, nipping at her skin with my teeth and soothing the small bites with my tongue. She let out a loud moan when I reached the sweet spot on her neck. In the distance, I heard some sort of buzzing or beeping, but I ignored it needing to feel more of Coral's skin.

"Li, wait," Coral panted as she shifted underneath me.

I finally came to my senses enough to realize she was trying to reach her phone. I sat up enough to let her reach her phone. She glanced at the screen and quickly glanced at me. I crinkled my brows knowing who it is. Out of pure jealousy, I reached for her phone to look at the screen. The name "Senator Nathaniel Roberts" flashed across the screen before Coral snatched the phone from my hand.

"*Hey beautiful,*" I mocked, repeating the text message he just sent. "Why is he still calling and texting you?" My tone was low, almost deadly.

"Leave it alone," Coral told me but that was not happening.

"Leave it alone?" I raised an eyebrow.

"Li, he's just a friend."

"A friend you've fucked. A friend who obviously wants more than to be just friends."

At this accusation, Coral pushed me fully off of her and sat up. "I don't have to explain any of my relationships to you," she pointed an accusatory finger at me.

"That's where you're wrong," I growled, and pulled her mouth to mine once again. I refused to release her lips as I stood us both up and back her towards the elevator. "He can't have you," I said in between the kisses I peppered along her lips and down her neck.

I pushed her back against the wall of elevator, and with my free hand I pressed the button for the second floor. I captured her lips again and moved my hand down to unbutton her jeans.

"Spread your legs," I commanded once I got the button undone. A small piece of me felt vindicated when she listened and did as I requested. I moved my hand inside her silky thong underwear to feel her already wet for me. "Does he make you wet like this?" I questioned, bringing my soaking wet finger up for her to see.

"What are you…?" she panted.

"Does he make you wet like this?" I barked out again at the same time I shoved my hand back into her wetness. With my mouth, I sucked on the side of her neck eliciting another moan. Her hips began to move against my hand. "That's it, CeCe. Ride my fingers," I encouraged as I flicked my index and middle fingers over her bulging clit. Moving lower, I let my fingers sink into her drenched pussy. Moving in and out, I spread her wetness all over her labia. Coral's hips began moving erratically and I knew her orgasm was within reach.

"Come on, CeCe. Come for me," I whispered in her ear and just like that she did. She came all over my hand. Those hazel eyes stared at me in wonder and satisfaction. But we were far from done. By the end of the night, this woman would know who she belonged to.

* * *

CORAL

"Daamn," I purred as I glanced down at his dark head bobbing up and down between my legs that were now spread eagle on his huge sleigh bed. Liam was clearly not playing games tonight. It took him precisely thirty seconds to strip both of us out of our clothes once we exited the elevator.

"Oh shiiit," I groaned as he wrapped his tongue around my clit at the same time his fingers made contact with my G-spot. I raised my hips to meet his hungry mouth, and Liam removed his fingers, placing a death grip around my thighs, keeping me from moving away from him. He began doing that damn circular movement with his tongue and I could no longer hold myself up. My head fell against the soft pillows and my orgasm crashed into me. My back arched off the bed and in the distance I heard loud moaning, only to realize it's my own voice.

When I finally opened my eyes, it was to see Liam leaning over me, staring intently. The look on his face was one of a hungry predator whose sole purpose in life at this moment was to claim his prey.

"Do you come for him like that?"

Still dazed from the fog of my previous orgasm it took a few seconds for Li's words to register. "Wh-what?" I asked, trying to steady my heartbeat, but it was too late. Before I could get the word out fully, I felt Liam's huge hardness already pushing inside me, as he propped my leg over his shoulder.

"I said do you come for him like that?!"

His voice was demanding. I couldn't respond as he leaned down and took one of my pert nipples into his mouth. I cupped the back of his head with one hand and thrust my breasts higher, pushing into his mouth. Liam picked up his pace as he thrust even faster in and out of my warm wetness. I grew even wetter from hearing the slap of his skin against mine. Pushing up, Li lifted his head, lowered my leg from his shoulder to wrap around his waist and stared down at me again. I used this opportunity to wrap my other leg around him and pump my hips meeting him stroke for stroke.

"Tell me," he groaned, while shifting his hips and speeding up even more so his cock came in contact with my G-spot on every down stroke.

I looked into his eyes and knew what he wanted me to say. I could tell by his insistence and the emotions in his eyes that he was claiming me. But I wouldn't say what he wanted to hear. I couldn't.

"Liam." I instead panted his name as he began rubbing circles over my clit with his thumb.

"Say it!" he demanded more harshly applying more pressure to my bulging pearl.

I could feel another orgasm was imminent. "Liam...don't stop," I barely got out as I wrapped my other leg even more tightly around his hip.

"Coral," his voice was low, guttural, a warning.

I could see the beads of sweat running down the side of his neck. Instead of giving him what he wanted, I reached up to lick the salty liquid and trail my tongue down towards his ear where I nipped his earlobe. "Make me come again," I whispered in his ear.

"Tell me what I want to hear," he responded, shifting his hips yet again.

"Ahhh," I cried out at the intensity of all the feelings rushing through my body. "Liiii," I half panted and half pleaded wanting the orgasm that was just out of reach. When I thought it was in reach, Liam pulled himself completely out of me. "Nooo," I cried out, pissed, but not for long.

Liam's strong hands were at my waist, flipping me over onto my stomach and pulling me up so I was on all fours. Just that quickly he was once again pushing inside of me. He kneed my legs even wider, thrusting so deeply that I couldn't catch my breath.

"Daaamn," I moaned. "Li, fuck me harder," I panted, getting lost in the feel of him so deep inside of me, his hands tightly gripped my waist, and his warm breath against the back of my neck.

"Say it, CeCe!" he continued to order.

I shook my head, silently refusing to give him what he wants.

"Grrr," he literally growled, pulling me up so my back was against his sweaty chest. Reaching down, he let his fingers rub against my clit and my head fell back against his shoulder at the sensation.

"Why are you so goddamn stubborn?!" he grunted in my ear. I

knew he was close to coming too. His hips began moving wildly. The only sounds that could be heard in the room were his grunts mixed with my moans and the slapping of flesh against flesh. It was the most erotic sound ever. The force of Li's thrust propelled me forward so much I had to grip onto the top of the headboard to keep from falling over. Liam was pounding into me so fiercely my fingers were getting smashed against the wall with each thrust. I knew I would have bruises in the morning.

Before I could move my hands, Liam leaned down over me, still pounding fiercely into me, running his hands along the length of my arms and down over my hands, shielding my hands from the impact of the wall. It was a move that was tender in spite of the ravenous way he was still hammering at my pussy with his huge stiffness. I closed my eyes and bit my bottom lip to keep from yelling out exactly what he wanted to hear. I refused to let him claim me, but that little show of protection was almost my undoing.

"*Ahhhh!*" I screamed out when my orgasm finally ripped into me.

"Fuck!" I heard Liam over my shoulder and felt his warm breathe like a caress at the back of my neck as he comes. I felt his hot liquid release into me. "He can't have you!" Li panted as he pulled out and released the rest of his come all over my lower back and buttocks.

I sighed at the feeling of his warm semen running down my back and ass, dripping onto my leg. I felt Liam's strong fingers, rubbing my ass cheeks and labia from behind and I realized he was massaging his come into me. Another act of claiming me as his. I fell down to the bed, laying on my stomach feeling all types of emotions I couldn't even begin to name.

"Li..." I called out when I felt him move off the bed.

"Don't move!" he ordered in his pissed off voice. I knew he was angry because I refused to say what he wanted to hear.

I watched his perfectly sculpted and rounded ass as he moved into the bathroom. I watched as he used the toilet and I licked my lips. I don't usually get turned on by watching my lovers use the toilet, but it was different with Li. Everything was different with him. I wanted to taste him. I went to sit up and felt his heavy hand pressing my back down.

"I said don't move." His voice was as unyielding as his hand on my back was.

I felt the wet, warm cloth glide over my back, butt, and in between my legs, cleaning me off.

"Turn over."

I did as instructed. I looked up at his perfectly chiseled jaw with the light stubble on it and noticed the tightness in it and his lowered eyelids.

"You're angry," I stated as an observation.

He merely looked at me, tossed the cloth on the nightstand, and moved in the bed behind me, pulling me so my back was against his chest. His one arm held my body tightly against him while he used the other to cradle my head. He tucked his head in the curve between my shoulder and neck.

"Go to sleep, CeCe." Those were the last words I heard before I drifted off into a peaceful rest.

CHAPTER 14

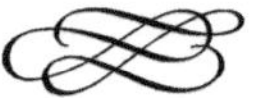

*L*iam

Yup, I was pissed as hell last night. I wanted Coral tell me she belonged to me. Was that too much to ask? Probably, but I could be a selfish bastard at times. Especially, considering I hadn't told her the reasons I left all those years ago. I could understand why she hesitated. Still, seeing that son of a bitch call and text her like he had rights to her did something to me. I might've been less jealous if she'd known where she belonged. Hell, that's a lie; I've hated Nathaniel for years because I knew he had a thing for her. I never liked any of her past boyfriends. Yet, I never felt threatened by any of them because I knew they would never know her the way I do.

I sighed as I ran my finger along her sleeping jaw. She looked so peaceful in my bed. As if in her sleep she knew it was where she belonged. If only she realized the same while she was awake. A knot formed in my stomach as I realized I'd have to leave her in a few hours to catch my flight.

"Mmmm. Why are you looking at me like that?" her eyes were barely open as she yawned, covering her mouth with one hand.

"I'm thinking how perfect you look naked in my bed."

"Oh, you're not still pissed at me?" she grinned.

"No, I'm still pissed. And you know why. If I didn't have a flight to catch, I'd show you how pissed again. Maybe I can delay my meetings?" I wondered out loud as I reached down in between her legs. "Are you sore?" I asked, knowing I had been a little heavy-handed the night before.

"It's fine."

That wasn't a "no" I realized. I pushed back the covers. "I ran you a bath," I said at the same time I pulled her into my arms. I carried her to the warm bath that I'd already filled with bath salts. I let her feet fall into the warm water and held her arms as she lowered herself into the bath. I held back a groan as I took in every inch of her naked body.

"Thank you," she said just above a whisper.

I leaned down on one knee next to the tub. "I'm sorry I didn't mean to—"

My apology was cut short when Coral cupped my face and pulled my lips in for a kiss. It was short, but enough to make me want to pull her out of this tub and take her back to bed.

"I'm fine," she stated after pulling back. "You didn't hurt me." She picked up one of my hands and pressed kisses to my own bruised knuckles. I remembered the bruises were from the headboard when I used my hands to cover hers. I would do anything to protect this woman from more pain.

She leaned back against the tub. "How long will you be gone?" she asked.

"Uh," I stuttered, distracted by her breasts that were barely covered by the water. "Um, tomorrow morning."

"Okay," she responded, closing her eyes.

I knew her mind was working on what she'd do with me gone. "I have Brian and Mitch coming over in the next half hour." I warned her in case she had any thoughts of going off on her own to work the case.

At that she opened one eyelid. "I expected nothing less. But it's only six am on a Saturday. You don't think they wanted to sleep in a little?"

I shrugged. "Your safety is more important than their sleep."

To that, she merely shook her head and closed her eyes.

I couldn't help it. I needed to touch her one last time before I left. Rolling up the sleeve of my shirt, I reached down into the water between her legs and felt for her swollen pearl.

"Open your eyes," I said low in her ear.

She listened without hesitation and looked directly at me, widening her legs granting me better access. When she bit her bottom lip moaning, I reached over and captured that lip myself. I nipped at it with my teeth, then used my tongue to soothe the mild bite. My tongue entered her mouth at the same time I slid my pointer and middle fingers into Coral's warm pussy. I used my thumb to grind her clit in a circular motion. My cock jumped when she let out a low moan and sighed. She pulled back and her head fell against the back of the tub. Her eyelids fluttered as she struggled to keep her eyes open, staring at me. I saw her knuckles turning red as she gripped the edges of the bathtub.

"Let me see you come one last time before I go," I said, low and deep. Just as the last word escaped my mouth, I felt a flush of liquid and her thighs tightened around my hand, locking it in place as she let out a loud moan. Water splashed around the tub, a few drops landing on my pants as Coral squirmed, eeking out the last sensations of her orgasm. When she relaxed, I withdrew my hand, sticking my fingers into my mouth as she silently watched me through lowered lids. I licked my fingers, and closed my eyes, savoring her flavor. I swear it was the sweetest taste I'd ever tasted on a woman. A flavor that only I would be relishing for the rest of my life.

I'd already decided by the end of this trip, Senator Nathaniel Roberts would know who Coral belonged to.

* * *

CORAL

"Mmmm!" I stretched and sighed, not wanting to move from this bed. After checking the clock on the nightstand, I realized it was been nearly two hours since Liam had left for his flight. After he left, I decided to go back to sleep for a little while. I swore since I'd been in this house I'd slept better than I had in the last five years. That thought scared the hell out of me. This place started to feel too much like...home.

I tossed that thought aside as I pushed the warm down comforter off me, also ignoring the feeling of loneliness that began to creep in knowing Liam wasn't here. I also missed Laura since she was at her grandparents' for the weekend. I hated to think I was becoming so attached to either one of them. I really needed to get refocused on the main reason I was here, which was to catch a ghost. Not play wife and stepmother or whatever the hell this was I had been doing the last couple of weeks.

I was pretty sure Brian was here somewhere lurking in the house. Liam had let him in just before he left. I picked up my cell to text Brian that I was going to go for a run. I walked into the bedroom I'd been sleeping in for the past week only to find that my clothes were missing. I checked the drawers and closet to be sure and yup, nothing was there. I started to pick up my phone to call Liam, but on a hunch I doubled back into his room to start checking drawers. The first drawer I opened, I found my neatly folded panties and bras. I closed that one and opened the next one finding my workout clothes and so on. At some point during the night, Liam brought all my clothing in his room and unpacked them in his dressers. It appeared he even bought a few items to replace the clothes destroyed in my hotel suite.

"I'm going to kill him," I mumbled to myself as I donned a pair of running leggings, sports bra, t-shirt, and running hoodie. I heard my phone beep from a text message.

Ready when you are.

It was Brian's response to my previous text. *Good.* A long run, finished up with some yoga was just what I needed before I showered and then began to unpack my clothes from Liam's room back to the guest room where I'd been sleeping. After that I planned on trying to track down the security guard Rodrigo. He'd been MIA for a few days and I definitely got the impression he knew we were on to him. I would call Ron to put someone on Rodrigo's home address around the clock, but Ron's with Liam and I knew he'd be the first person Ron went to about this. The last thing I wanted was more of Liam trying to get me to back off this case.

"'Bout time you got up. I was starting to think you'd sleep till noon," Brian joked as I dismounted the stairs.

"Just resting up getting ready to dust you on this run," I retorted, adjusting the laces of my Nike running shoes.

"Don't threaten me with a good time."

I couldn't help but laugh at that. I'd seen a lot of vets who'd had horrific injuries and had such a difficult time getting their life back. There were even a few I knew who took their own lives due to the PTSD that can settle in after war. I was glad to see that Brian was not only physically capable as he was prior to the war, but that he still maintained his sense of humor.

"Let's go," I said, heading towards the door. I decided against going to the usual trail I ran. Instead I ran around the sprawling community that Li's house resided in. I took the opportunity to take in the surroundings. It was really a nice little community. I noticed a few families out and about with their children. I thought about how in just a few years these kids would likely be in the same classes as Laura when they started school. After some time thinking about that, I shook those thoughts remembering the purpose of this run was to get my mind off Liam and his daughter. I had to figure out what I needed to do to wrap this case up, find out who Ghost was, eliminate him, and move on with my life. Unfortunately, the very thought of wrapping the case up and leaving Liam caused a weight to settle in my chest as if a boulder were sitting on it. I was so caught off guard by this feeling that I slowed down to a light jog, cutting the run short after only five miles.

"You getting soft on me?" Brian's teasing voice taunted a little ahead of me.

I threw him a half smile. "Time for some yoga," I answered. We made our way back to the house and down to Liam's state of the art gym. Pulling out a mat I removed my sneakers and sat quietly on the mat. I heard Brian move around, eventually sitting next to me. He'd told me how a yoga practice helped him not only come to terms with his new body, but also stave off flashbacks in the early months and years of his recovery. We silently moved through a series of poses and sequences for the next forty-five minutes.

As we folded up our mats and cleaned up the gym, I turned my phone back on to see I had a few voice messages. I frowned wondering who it could be, my brain immediately working overtime thinking that Stacey, Liam, or Tasha were injured. I didn't recognize the number from the missed call, but as I checked my message I heard Susan, Laura's grandmother.

"Coral, I'm sorry, I got your number from Liam yesterday. An emergency has come up. Laura is fine, but John and I have to go out of town to check on our son and we need to drop Laura off before we leave…" I didn't waste time listening to the rest of the message. I hit the call back button and Susan answered after two rings.

"Susan hi, is everything okay?" I asked, worried. "Okay, I'm sorry to hear that. Sure, it's no problem," I responded to Susan's quick fire responses and explanation. By the time I hung up the phone, Brian was staring at me with a curious expression.

"Laura's grandparents have to go out to California to check on their son who was in a car accident. He's okay but in the hospital. They need to cut Laura's weekend short. They'll be here in a few minutes."

As soon as I finished explaining, the buzzer for the front gate rang. As we got to the front door, we saw on the monitor it was Laura with her grandparents. Within minutes, Laura had been dropped off and her grandparents had rushed off to go tend to their ailing son. Laura's huge green eyes stared up at me in wide-eyed innocence. Those eyes reminded me so much Liam's, I couldn't help the swell of emotion in my chest as I knelt to get eye level with her.

"Your daddy had to take a little trip, so it's just me and you until he gets back. Is that okay with you, Princess?" I asked, unzipping and removing her jacket.

"Yes," she nodded. "But can we call Daddy?"

"We sure can," I told her pulling out my phone. I pressed Li's number and after a few rings, it went to voicemail. I quickly explained what happened and assured him that Laura was okay. Then I gave her the phone so she could leave a voicemail.

"Hi Daddy! Nana and Papa had to go take care of Uncle Mike. I'm home with Ms. Coral. I'll be really good. I promise! Bye." Laura handed me back the phone and I said bye before hanging up.

"Alright, how about you play a game of hide-and-seek with Uncle Brian, while I go and get dressed and then maybe we can go to the community center?" I suggested, looking between Laura and Brian.

When they both nodded, and Brian covered his eyes and started counting, I began backing out of the room. The last sight I saw was Laura frantically searching for a good hiding space in the huge living room. I covered my mouth to stifle my laughter at the jovial sound. As I rushed through my shower and changed into a pair of skinny jeans and an off the shoulder, long-sleeve t-shirt, all my previous plans I had for this day fell by the wayside.

CHAPTER 15

*L*iam

"Show me what you've got so far," I told Randy as we met in some seedy, dive bar in the outskirts of Austin. I'd told Ron and my other security I needed them to meet with my father's security team to go over any security issues. The truth was, I needed this time alone to meet with Randy. He worked as my father's chief of staff, but in actuality he had been keeping tabs on my father's dealings for me over the years. My father slept with Randy's first wife some years ago to steal secrets about his company and he didn't realize Randy knew about it. Randy had been looking for a way to pay him back and I happened to be in the right place at the right time.

"I had my PI take these," Randy said pulling out a folder and opening it.

Inside the folder was picture after picture of my father plain as day fucking some younger woman. I was willing to bet good money this woman was hired specifically to fuck my father. My lips turned down in disgust at the images. I wasn't shocked. I had known my father had a penchant for prostitutes for years now. My mother had known as well. Hell, half the politicians and high level businessmen in this country did and while the general public probably wouldn't take too kindly to the governor of a major state paying for sex, it wasn't enough to destroy my father. With this evidence he'd probably finish out his tenure as governor and return as chairman of the board of Bennett Industries. I wouldn't have that. I knew he was into deeper shit than fucking a few prostitutes.

"This isn't enough, Ran. Have you checked the donors like I told you?"

Randy's balding head bobbed up and down as he nodded. "Yeah, but it's a dead end. All the donors appear to be on the up and up," he let out a long breath, clearly frustrated.

"Send me the list of donors and all their contributions. I have someone in mind who can trace money," I told him. "I'm going to keep these for insurance as well," I said picking up the folder and placing it in my briefcase. "We need more," I said, looking sternly into Randy's face as I stood. I'd been gone for nearly an hour and I needed to make it back downtown for the second leg of this trip.

"You never told me why you want this so bad." Randy's eyebrows raised as he stood as well. "I know what I have against your father. But what about you? He's your father, albeit he probably wasn't all that great, but why do you want to take him down so badly?"

In all of our years working together, Randy had never asked this question. I guessed it was because now I was the most adamant I had ever been on taking down my father. "Same reason as you. He tried to take the most important thing in my life from me. He's a controlling, manipulative son of a bitch who thinks he has the power and influence to out maneuver everyone."

I'd never told anyone besides Jeremy the whole story of how my father manipulated me into taking over Bennett Industries and marrying a woman I wasn't in love with, so that he could run for governor. The memory of it still made me blind with fury and it was why I'd spent the last five years trying to dig up every little secret on my father to take him down. I hadn't gathered the ammo I needed to rightfully dethrone him just yet, but I was close. I could feel it. I had a gut feeling this issue with Larry's murder and Bennett Industries' shady financial dealings from the past would lead right back to my father. Regrettably, that moment would have to wait a little while longer as I had another pressing issue I needed to handle.

I checked my watch, shook hands with Randy, and caught a cab back to the downtown office where I left Ron and my security. I alerted Ron there'd been a change of plans as we packed to head to the hotel. Instead of staying overnight in Austin, I called my pilot and scheduled a quick trip to our lovely nation's capital.

"D.C?" Ron's face was a picture of surprise and dismay.

"Yeah, DC? Is that a problem? You had other plans?" I asked, defensively.

He quickly changed his tone. "No, no it's just I wasn't expecting this. To better serve you, it's important that I, as head of your security, know what is happening."

I tilted my head to the side, and squinted, looking intensely at Ron. "So, me changing my schedule is a problem for you? Is that what you're saying? Because if it is—"

"No, no. I didn't mean anything like that."

"Good. Because I would hate to have to find another head of security. Someone who is more capable of keeping up with my changing plans." I lifted an eyebrow in warning. I didn't kid around when it came to security. "Let's make this the last time we ever have to have this type of conversation." And with that, I strolled off to towards the town car waiting to deliver us to our flight.

* * *

"Do you have an appointment?" the middle-aged grey-haired woman asked, looking up from her appointment book.

I gave her my warmest smile. "No, but I'm sure Senator Roberts will see me," I stated, confidently. "Just tell him an old friend is here to see him." That's right; I went to see the punk who kept sniffing around what belonged to me. United States Senator or not, I wasn't about to let him think he had some type of chance that he never actually did.

"And your name? Mr.?"

"Bennett. CEO of Bennett Industries." I was not above throwing my name and title around to get what I wanted. There were some traits I learned from my father that I managed to hold onto. Luckily, I wasn't a bastard like he was. At least, I'd like to think not.

"Oh, Mr. Bennett. Of course. One second." Her whole demeanor changed hearing my name. You couldn't run a huge company like I did and not have your name well known in D.C. circles.

I nodded, took a few steps back, and pulled my phone out of my pocket. I saw I had a few voicemails, missed calls and text messages. I checked voicemails first and heard that Laura's grandparents had to end their weekend with her early because Mike had been in a car accident. I smiled absentmindedly as I heard the message from my little girl and Coral, assuring me that she was okay. Next, I opened my text messages and laughed out loud at the funny-faced pictures Coral had sent me of the two of them. Apparently, they had spent the day at the community center with Brian and Mitch, and then Coral took them for a spa day. I frowned at the pictures she sent me of Laura's little painted nails and toes.

You let my baby get red nail polish? I texted Coral.

But I was only teasing. I was extremely relieved to see the two of them having so much fun together. Within seconds my phone was chimed with a response.

Relax, daddy. It'll come off in a few days and we're waiting a few weeks until we get the tattoos and tongue piercing.

I laughed out loud causing everyone, including Ron, to stop and stare at me. I didn't have time to respond before Nathaniel's pompous ass appeared at his door. My frown immediately returned. I took one last look at the pictures, reassuring myself that it was my home Coral was at and not his.

"Liam, well isn't this an...unexpected surprise," he said as he stepped fully out of his office, extending his hand for a handshake.

We shook hands and for a few seconds, sized each other up. "I bet it is," I returned. He was only an inch shorter than my six-foot three frame, and about as muscular as I was.

"Why don't we take this in my office?" He stepped back and allowed me to pass through to his office. When Ron attempted to follow me in, I held up my hand. "I'll be fine, Ron. You can wait out here."

I heard the door close behind me as I looked around Nate's office. It was the typical office of any Junior Senator. Pictures with the President and other important dignitaries lined the shelves, books, and papers stacked on his huge desk. From the window one could make out the Lincoln Memorial in the distance. In all honesty, Nate was a pretty good Senator. His ideals were progressive enough and he had really done some good things for the people of his state. Still, fuck him. He'd set his sights on something that belonged to me.

"I can't say I'm all that surprised to see you. I was wondering when you'd make an appearance. Considering..."

Considering I was fucking your soulmate. I knew that's what he wanted to say and my hands instantly curled into fists.

"Considering...you want something that doesn't belong to you."

I took a step towards him but stopped myself. Nate didn't appear all that flustered by my appearance at his office. He planted his feet and stuck his hands in the pockets of his Armani suit pants, giving the image of someone who was relaxed, but I knew better. We had the same type of training.

"*Belong?*" he raised a questioning brow.

"You heard me."

"I doubt that's how Coral would see it."

"I doubt you understand most things when it comes to Coral."

"Care to enlighten me, Liam?"

I smiled at this pompous motherfucker. If this were any other circumstance, Nate was probably someone you'd want on your team. But I never liked him for the very reason I was standing here right now.

"How about this for enlightenment: Stop calling her. Stop texting her. Don't even think about her. Consider Coral a distant, fond memory you'll *never* get the opportunity to make new memories with."

By the time I'd finished talking, I realized my heart rate had sped up and the rising and falling of my chest as it expanded with each inhale. My body was on high alert. I couldn't stand this asshole and I knew it was because he'd seen Coral naked. I didn't care to imagine how many times they'd been together, where, or what other parts of herself she'd shared with him. It wasn't even so much the thought of what they shared physically, it was the very thought that Coral and Nate could have had a very real connection. Images of her lying in his arms as she shared parts of her life that she'd only told me was what truly pissed me off. Sex could be intimate, but letting down those walls and letting someone know the heart, your fears, and what kept you up at night was real intimacy. That was type of intimacy I'd only shared with Coral and I shuddered to think she'd had that with someone else.

He pointed a finger at himself. "Are you giving *me* an order, Liam?" he asked, as his chest rose and fell as rapidly as mine.

"Not an order, Senator. We're no longer in the military. Just think of it as some friendly advice from one vet to another." I smiled, but there was no hint of kindness in it. I stepped closer. "You're barking up the wrong tree. Hell, I don't even blame you. One can't help but fall in love with Coral. She's smart as a whip, able to kick the ass of most men twice her size which also makes her sexy as hell. Not to mention that she handles a glock almost as well as I do. She's the total package. *My* total package. It's time for you to find your own." With that, I stepped around Nate to head towards the door. I'd made my point.

"You keep talking about her like she's some prized possession of yours. If you knew anything about Coral you'd know she wouldn't appreciate anyone thinking they have some sort of ownership over her." His voice had a haughty intonation to it that frazzled my damn nerves.

"If I knew anything about her," *This shithead thinks he just one upped me.* I slammed the door to his office, and within a few long strides I was directly in his face. We were chest to chest, glaring at one another. "You think you fucking know her because you've seen her naked a few times?" I seethed in his face. "You think you know her because, what? You know where she went to college or you shared a few drinks after engaging in gunfire, once upon a time years ago halfway around the world?"

I was now poking his chest with my finger, trying to refrain from using my hands to do some real damage in his office. "You only know what she let you know. You have no idea how far she has gone to protect the people she loves. I do. You have no idea that Whitney Houston is her favorite singer because it's who her mother adored until her dying day. You weren't the person she called at three am crying afraid she'd failed her sister when her ballet career ended. That was me!"

I slapped my chest with my hand for emphasis. "You have no fucking clue what a bastard her father was to her and that it made her who she is today. You. don't. know. shit. about. her." I poked his chest with each word. "And most importantly, you're not whose name she was calling out last night. Or the man who she will spend the rest of her life with. That's me. And I don't care whose head I have to take off to make that happen. I've already plotted on my own blood. I have no problem making you next. Don't fuck with me."

I finally stepped back, my fists clenched with anger at my sides. It was time for me to go. I turned to leave without another word. My last image was Nate standing stone silent, half-stunned, half-angered as the truth of my words sunk in. What I said in there went for him, my father, and anyone else who had notions of getting in the way of Coral and I. Hell, that included Coral's stubborn ass too.

* * *

CORAL

"Hey kid, how about we clean up and then watch a movie?" I suggested to Laura as she sat across the table from me. We were finishing up our dinner of peanut butter and jelly sandwiches. It's not the best dinner, but I hated cooking and it was quick and easy.

"Can we watch the Little Mermaid?" she asked in wide-eyed excitement.

And for some reason I couldn't say no to this little person even if I wanted to. "Yup, but you have to help with the dishes first, okay?"

"Kay!" she clapped her hands, dancing in her chair at the prospect of watching her favorite movie.

We finished our dinner and I poured some milk for Laura to go with the chocolate chip cookies that we bought from a bakery, and then headed into the family room. I pulled up the Little Mermaid as Laura sat at her little table and ate her cookies and milk. She delightfully sang along to all the songs she'd committed to memory. We were about three-quarters of the way through the movie when Laura came over and sat on the leather couch next me. Before I knew it, she had made her way into my lap and had fallen fast asleep just as the ending credits began to roll. It was a feeling of contentment I hadn't had in a long time and emotion began to rise up from the pit of my stomach.

Instead of getting up and immediately taking Laura to her room, I decided to call Tasha. It'd been a few days since we last talked.

"Hey," she answered.

"Hey, you busy?"

"No, what's up?"

"Why does something have to be up?"

"I can hear it in your voice. You sound...I don't know contemplative or something."

"Since when the hell did I become so easy to read?" I started to question my reputation for not being able to be read by others. I was the one who picked up on body language and tone. Not others.

"You're not. It's just sometimes you let your guard down around certain people. Me...Liam."

I sighed, wanting to refute her words but I couldn't. It was why I called in the first place.

"Speaking of which, how is Liam?" Tasha asked.

"Out of town. But Laura's here with me," I said, looking down at the peacefully sleeping toddler in my lap. I hadn't even noticed my hand stroking her hair until just then.

"He left her there with you?" Tasha's voice rose a few levels in surprise.

"Not intentionally."

"So, when are you going to admit it?"

My head jerked back in surprise at the sudden question. "Admit what?" I asked although I had an idea of what she was going to say.

"Oh okay, we're playing this game?"

"Tasha," I warned.

"When are you going to admit you're still in love with that man and that you've even fallen for his daughter? Why haven't you asked him what happened all those years ago and why he left and for God's sake when are you going to let him make an honest woman out of you so you can stop running all over the world fighting God knows who for God knows what?"

I opened and closed my mouth a few times attempting to make a biting comeback but the smart retort didn't come. They were simple questions really, but ones I had been avoiding. I'd been focusing so hard on finding Ghost and figuring out who was behind the death of Li's employee, in part because espionage and death threats didn't scare me. That came easy. It was emotions like love and heartbreak that scared the shit out of me. Also, I was a firm believer in not asking questions if I didn't want to hear the truthful answers. I wasn't sure if I wanted to hear the real reason why Li left.

"Tasha," I said in a whisper, both to not disturb Laura, and because I was still trying to formulate some type of answer.

"Why?" she asked again.

"I'm not ready for the answers yet," I admitted. "You of all people know what that feels like." It might've been a little bit of a low blow, but I decided to go there. I wasn't the only one who's holding back on uncomfortable truths.

"I was wondering when you'd go there," she said, her voice flat. "I just don't know." She sighed, obviously frustrated.

"I know. I just can't help worry about you. What if something happens to me? I don't want you to not have anyone. You could at least let me tell Stacey," I pounced on a moment of weakness.

"I'll make a deal with you," she answered.

"No. I don't make deals," I frowned.

"Aww come one. Look, if you at least consider taking the plunge and asking Liam about what happened five years ago and then really opening up about your feelings for one another, I will consider talking with Stacey. Okay?" I heard the hope in Tasha's voice and I wouldn't say no to her this time.

It really was one of the biggest fears of mine, leaving Tasha behind if something were to happen to me. She didn't have friends. She had no family ties and she spent her days writing, which earned her a living and fed her creative passion. But, outside of that, she had no life to speak of.

"It's a deal," I said, finally.

"Okay, you go put little Laura to bed. We'll talk soon."

"Oh, speaking of, did I tell you that Laura loved the part when Danica finally retrieves the sacred seed from the evil governor? She can't wait to read the next book, or have it read to her."

"Awww, give that little munchkin a kiss for me and tell her Danica is coming back strong."

"Will do. Bye," I said quietly, as I hung up the phone. I picked up Laura and cradled her in both arms to take her up the stairs when I remembered the elevator next to the staircase. I pressed the button, peeking at Laura to make sure she wasn't awakened by the sound of the doors opening. She stirred a little bit but remained sleep. Once in her room, I removed her shoes and changed her into her favorite My Little Pony nightgown. I knew we were not going to get any reading done, so, I placed her in the bed, turned on her night light that lit up stars and shapes around the room and then go to tuck her in. As soon as I began pulling up the covers, Laura's little hand grabbed mine.

"Can you stay with me?" her cute little voice requested and I was putty in her hands.

"Sure, sweetheart," I crooned, as I eased in the bed, lying down next to her. I figured I'd stay for another five or ten minutes until she got back to sleep. I made a short mental list of what I needed to clean up in the family room before the world went black and I fall into a deep slumber.

CHAPTER 16

*L*iam

I was fucking exhausted. After that little showdown with Nate earlier, I headed to dinner with a few of my DC connections. I also had some of them digging to gather dirt on my father. His connections were long and his reach wide, but I knew he had some massive dirt buried somewhere. After dinner, I made the decision to hop on the plane and head back home to my women. It was now three in the morning and I was dead on my feet.

I sighed and ran my hand through my hair, dropping my suitcase and briefcase by the door. I'd already texted Brian and told him no need to come over today since I was back home. I headed up the stairs to first go check on my baby girl and then to my room where I hoped to find Coral. I knew by now she'd seen that I moved all her clothing and items to my bedroom. I wondered why she hadn't said anything, but then I figured it was because she was busy with Laura all day. I made my way down the hall to Laura's room and pushed open the slightly ajar door, and the sight before me left me stunned.

I eased in quietly to not disturb the scene before me. I stood at the foot of Laura's bed with my heart on my sleeve as I watched Coral and Laura sleeping peacefully. Coral was laying on her side, as Laura's little body was tucked in close, facing her, with her little arm wrapped around Coral's waist and her other arm wrapped around her favorite stuffed bear. Coral's arm was protectively draped over Laura.

I took a few more moments to digest the scene. Needing to capture this moment, I pulled out my phone and snapped a couple of pictures. I looked through a few and chose my favorite to make my phone's wallpaper. Afterwards, I strolled over to the far side of the bed and reached down to pull the covers up over Laura. Before I could even graze her shoulder with my fingers, my wrist was caught in a vise grip. I looked down to see a mocha colored hand gripping my wrist. I couldn't help but smile.

"Easy, Scorpion. It's just Papa Bear checking on his cub," I murmured.

Coral slowly opened her eyelids and those alert hazel eyes zoned in on me. Realization quickly settled in and she let my wrist go.

"I fell asleep," she half-whispered. She looked amazed that she'd spent the night in here.

"I see that. Why don't we give your ribs a rest and let Princess finish sleeping by herself. You come with me," I said, grinning down at Laura's knee braced against Coral's ribcage.

She squinted as she looked down and frowned. "I think I'm going to have bruises. I'm sure she socked me in the eye at least once," she halfheartedly groaned, rising slowly from the miniature bed.

I frowned knowing how rough my daughter could be in her sleep, and the soreness that accompanied, sleeping in such a small bed all night. "Come on," I said once I re-covered Laura who was still resting peacefully.

"I'm not sleeping in your room," Coral grumbled groggily even though she's letting me lead her out the room and down the hall.

Of course, I had no intention of letting her sleep anywhere else besides my bed. Thankfully, she didn't put up much more of a fuss as we entered my bedroom.

"Lay down," I told her, pulling the sheets back and pushing her towards the mattress.

She fell willingly and I removed the ankle boots she still had on.

Leaving her side for a second I searched through drawers trying to remember which one I'd placed her sleeping clothes in. Finally finding it, I pulled out a t-shirt and shorts. It took some maneuvering, but I managed to get her out of her jeans and button up shirt. I inadvertently licked my lips at the sight of the top of her breasts peeking out of her bra. Instinctively, I leaned down and placed a kiss on her cheek, neck and top of each breast. Coral sighed and stirred a little, but her eyes remain closed. Even though she appeared completely relaxed and asleep, I knew she was only letting me do this because she was comfortable with me. With the instincts of a cat, she'd be out of this trance in a millisecond if she sensed danger. That thought both comforted and terrified me. I was grateful to know Laura was with someone so capable and loving in my absence, but it also reminded me of how much fighting this woman had to do in her life.

When I finished changing her, I undressed, stripping down to by boxer briefs and climbed in bed next to Coral, pulling her close to me so we were face to face. I settled in and smiled in satisfaction when I felt Coral scoot even closer into my embrace. I reached over to turn the lamp on the nightstand off, and resettle myself in.

The quiet of the room was disturbed when Coral announced, "I'm moving back in the guest room first thing in the morning." Seconds before drifting off back to sleep.

"If you say so," I said, placing another kiss to her forehead and pulling her even tighter into my side.

* * *

CORAL

"We found him!" I exclaimed, as I barged through Liam's office door with Brian right on my heels. We'd been searching for the last week for Rodrigo, the security guard. I'd gone over his interview numerous times, picking up on the subtle body movements that signaled he was lying. He knew a lot more than he was willing to let on. And since the owner of the junkyard identified him as the man who tried to get in to see Larry's damaged car, I knew he was the key to solving this case.

Liam's head jerked up from his computer screen in surprise. It took less than a second for his eyes to widen with the realization of who I was referring to. By then, I stood in front of his desk with my opened tablet showing a Google maps image of a nightclub that existed just outside of Dallas.

"Here?" Liam asked, looking between Brian and I.

"Turns out, Rodrigo's cousin is Antonio Vegara, owner of the Onyx Nightclub. Rodrigo's hiding out, staying at the apartment that resides just above the club and acting as security for the club. Antonio's on the up and up, so it's doubtful he knows what his cousin is into or that we're looking for him."

Liam nodded in understanding. "'Kay, so we need to go speak to Rodrigo. It's Friday which means he's probably going to be busy working security at the club tonight."

"Go ahead and tell him your plan for this one," Brian intervened, shaking his head as if he already knows Liam's reaction.

I side-eyed Brian, silently telling him to shut the hell up, but he just smirked knowingly. I rolled my eyes and turned again to face Liam. "Alright so, I'm going to go in the club and speak with him. You know; ask a couple of questions. Get the information we need," I explained, greatly downplaying my plans.

Liam didn't buy it for a second. Tilting his head to the side he glared at me. "You're going to use yourself as bait?" he asked rising from his chair.

"Not quite as bait. I mean, I probably will have to do a little...finessing to get him alone and whatnot, but..." I trailed off at the murderous look that passed over Liam's face.

"You thought I'd be okay with this?!" he thundered, looking straight at Brian.

"Listen," I said growing agitated at being overlooked.

"No, *you* listen," Liam now refocused his attention on me, "I told you I didn't want you walking into danger for this fucking case. I already have two Goddamn bodyguards on you at all times. Why the hell did you think I'd be okay with you walking the middle of some nightclub surrounded by hundreds of unknown people, wearing God knows what, to seduce some lowlife we know had something to do with Larry's death. No, this shit is not happening. Think of another way to get to him." The finality in his tone was supposed to make me think it was the end of the conversation. Not happening.

I smiled at Brian over my shoulder. "Brian, can you excuse us?"

Warily, he looked between me and Liam and finally, dipped his head in agreeance, leaving Liam and I alone.

"You know, there's not very many people I let talk to me like that. Don't let the fact that I woke up in your bed this morning get you too comfortable," I finished, returning the same stare he was giving me.

"Don't get cute, Coral. This is not happening. You're not using yourself as bait. Find another way to get to him." With that, he took his seat and started slamming folders and other items around his desk.

"This is happening, Liam whether you agree or not. Rodrigo is the key to this. I can feel it. Jabari's still having trouble accessing the content on the drive and getting Rodrigo is our last alternative. The sooner we get this done the better. You and I both know this is our best shot at ending this." I couldn't believe I was standing there pleading my case to Liam. Any other time I wouldn't give a shit whether or not someone agreed with my methods as long as I got the job done. I sighed, running my hand through my short curls, in an attempt to stave off my growing anger at how far this situation between Liam and I had gotten. I should have known there was no way I could take this case and not become personally invested. Now, I was waking up in his bed every damn morning, after helping tuck his daughter in at night.

"This has gotten too out of control," I said out loud, more to myself than to Liam.

Something in my tone must have caught Liam off-guard because he paused his little tirade and looked at me questioningly. "What are you talking about?"

Those green eyes that held so much emotion stared at me and that warm feeling in my chest that I had become accustomed to in the last few weeks started up again. I blew out a breath. "This," I waved my hand between the two of us. "I didn't come here for this. I came to work this case and get information I needed for another matter," I said being elusive. "I wasn't...this wasn't supposed to happen. It's been five years!" My voice was rising, the emotion bubbling over. "You left me. No explanation. No apologies. Just some pathetic note that I still don't know the meaning of. And I don't care." I held up my hand to stop whatever he was about to say. "Now, I'm waking up in your bed. Tucking your daughter in at night like some...I didn't come here to fall in..." I stopped not letting those words fall from my mouth. I stepped back from him, as he rounded his desk, reaching out for me.

"No," I fervently said, stepping back even more. "I'm doing this. I'm going to find out who the hell Rodrigo is working for and I will find whoever killed Larry and I will get the answers I need with or without your approval. *That* is what I'm here for." I took one last look at Liam's now forlorn expression and quickly strode out the door, slamming it behind me. I didn't even stop when I heard something crashing against Liam's office door behind me. Nor, did I stop as Brian's quick footsteps fell behind me.

"We're going for a run. Then we're going to spar," I threw over my shoulder as I opted to take the steps down the twenty-five flights instead of waiting for the elevator.

"I figured," Brian grumbled behind me.

CHAPTER 17

Liam

This Goddamn woman, I thought as she descended the stairs covered in a too tight, too short, black dress. The front was covered in a black shimmery material, but the sleeves, sides and from what I could see, the back were made of a sheer black material, exposing the fact that she was not wearing a bra or panties under this thing. The dark, smoky eye makeup and dangly earrings all gave an alluring look to the outfit, but what completely set it off was Coral's toned legs on full display in the pair of "come fuck me" heels she was wearing. The heels had to be at least five inches and every time she moved, the muscles in her legs and ass bulged and flexed to perfection, causing a stirring in my loins. Even though I was still pissed as hell at her, I had to tuck my hands in my pockets to keep them off of her. For now.

This insane woman hadn't spoken to me since she stormed out of my office earlier today. I was so pissed when she slammed my door, I threw my very heavy glass paperweight against it, causing it to shatter. Maintenance had to spend several hours cleaning up shards of broken glass and the dent in the door. To say my employees were all shocked was an understatement. I didn't lose my cool like that. Not ever. Except when it came to her. It was then I made a decision…well, a few decisions. The first being that there was no way she was going to walk into that club without me nearby. She wasn't doing this alone. The second decision was that I would finally tell her why I'd left all those years ago. I would confess what really went down, explain why I did what I had to do and then make her understand that her place was and always has been with me.

"What do you think?" she asked as she spun around giving everyone an eye full.

I squeezed my hands into fists when I heard someone behind me whistle low in appreciation. Ron, Brian, Mitch and a few more of my security staff were there to accompany Coral to the club. It might've been overkill but was the only way I felt comfortable going into this.

"You look great, Coral. No doubt you'll catch Rodrigo's eye," Brian said as he put his hand on my shoulder.

I cut my eyes at him trying to figure out if he was trying to calm me down or egg me on.

"You're sure he has no idea who you are?" I asked, moving my gaze from Brian to Coral. I saw her breasts rise and fall as she sighed heavily, clearly annoyed by my question.

"I'm sure your team explained this to you already." She barely looked at me.

"They have, but I want *you* to explain it to me," I ordered, stepping directly in her line of sight so she had nowhere to look but up at me. I planted my feet and fold my arms over my chest waiting impatiently for her to reassure me of this plan.

She ran her hands through her fluffed curls, affixed her earrings and smoothed the sides of her dress before she looked me in the eye again. "Rodrigo never met me. All the interviews were done through Ron," she gestured to Ron who remained quiet on the other side of the room. "I was always in a separate room, and Rodrigo worked the night shift, so he was never at the office at the same time I was since I've always been there during the day. Only the people in this room know I've been working this case. So, you can relax and let me do my damn job." Her face was a hard mask of impatience and agitation.

I stepped closer, peering down at her. "The fact that you're in that slinky ass dress and not locked up in my bedroom is proof I'm letting you do your damn job," I said low enough for her ears only. I watched as her chest heaved and the small vein in her neck quickened ever so slightly, revealing my words have the desired effect on her.

"I'm going to kick your ass one day," she growled lowly.

"I'm looking forward to it. Let's get this over with." I stated the second part loud enough so everyone in the room hears it, as I gripped Coral's arm and lead her out the room.

This woman was going to be the death of me, I kept thinking to myself as I watched her dress rise up almost showing her entire ass as she bent to get into the car. It's going to be a long damn night.

* * *

CORAL

This man was going to be the death of me.

This was all I could think as I strutted my way through the club, but felt his eyes on my every move just as much as if he were touching me. As far as plans and assignments went, this one was relatively easy. My goal was to simply make contact with Rodrigo, entice him a little, and get him into one of the private rooms. Once there, I'd plug him for information. I knew he was there at the office the night of Larry's death. He had to have known or seen something, if he knew enough to go to the junkyard and start asking questions.

I scanned the club and there were hundreds of people here. The bass of some techno-mix was playing loudly and the strobe lights made it difficult to focus on any one spot for too long. Luckily, I'd already prepared for all of this. I knew exactly where Rodrigo was positioned in the club. His spot, I'd been informed by our contact, was posted up by the hallway that leads to a number of rooms where patrons could pay to have some privacy for however long. I looked up to the second level where there were many scantily dressed women and men pushing up on them, dancing. I spotted one of the new security guards Liam had brought. Most of the rest, including Ron, were waiting outside. Rodrigo knew who they are and would likely suspect something if he saw them.

Instead of making my way over to Rodrigo, I strutted over to the bar. I smiled at the young, perky bartender. "Rum and coke, Sweetie."

"Coming up," she beamed, as she made her way down the bar to prepare the drink.

I watched as it was made. She slid the drink down the bar and I caught it with one hand, and pulled out a few bills out of the top of my dress with the other. Winking at her I paid for the drink and her tip. I brought the drink up to my lips and the smell automatically made my stomach roll in protest. I hated the smell, taste, and even the thought of alcohol. I've hated it ever since I was a kid and I would smell the stench of alcohol on my father as he used me as his personal punching bag, then forced me to get up and make him another drink. Usually, I was able to mask my distaste of alcohol when I needed to for a case, but it was harder for some reason this time.

"Shit!" I exclaimed as someone bumped into me spilling my drink. Only my quick instincts allowed me to avoid spilling it on my dress.

"You didn't want that shit anyway," a low, familiar and comforting voice said in my ear.

My lips curled up into a smile of gratitude as Liam sat on the stool next to me, keeping his head turned away so no one saw his face or that he was talking to me. I watched out of the corner of my eye as he gestured for the bartender and leaned over whispering something to her. She scurried off with a crisp $100 bill in her hand, made another drink that looked like the one I had just spilled and brought it to me.

"Here you go, hon," she winked at me and then moved to the next customer.

"You can drink this one," I heard Li say before he rose from the stool. "I've got my eyes on you," he said before disappearing into the crowd. I sniffed this drink and there was no alcohol smell to it. I sipped and realized it's just regular coke. I could have sworn I saw the bartender pour rum into the drink. I realized Li must have paid her off to make it look like she put alcohol in it I thought as I casually sipped my drink looking around the club. I finally let my eyes rest on the area I knew Rodrigo was in. I feigned as if I was just looking around, until I made eye contact with him. When he saw me, I tossed him my most flirtatious smile then looked down again, taking another sip of my drink. After a few more moments I raised my lashes and looked right at Rodrigo, to see if I still had his attention. When I saw I did, I smiled again, placed my drink on the bar, and headed to the dance floor.

As luck would have it, Beyonce's "Flawless" remix featuring Nicki Minaj came on and I let myself get into the song. I grabbed the closest guy to me. He was actually an inch or so shorter than me in these heels, but not bad looking with his rich caramel skin. Unfortunately, he tried to talk and almost singed my eyelashes with his breath. I placed my finger over his mouth, shushing him. "Just enjoy," I crooned as I turned and began grinding on him to the beat of the music. I looked up to see if Rodrigo was still watching me, and I put a little more emphasis on it, turning to give him a nice view of my ass as I held my breath and continued to dance.

As soon as the song ended I made my way off the dance floor, ignoring my dance partner's pleas for a second dance. I focused intently on Rodrigo, as I strutted slowly over to him. I watched as he eyed me up and down, licking his lips.

"Hello," I whispered, breathily, looking up into his dark brown eyes. "Want to dance?"

He gave me another once over and bit his lower lip. "I-I can't leave my post, beautiful." His voice was laced with regret.

"Oh, are you working?" I asked in my perfect minx voice, trailing my finger up and down his muscular chest.

"I'm security."

I got close and whispered in his ear. "Well, you definitely deserve a little something for keeping us all safe," I said, sliding my hand down his stomach. Suddenly, Rihanna's "Pour it Up," began playing and I smiled devilishly at him. I pulled him towards the dance floor. He gave minor resistance but then followed. Once in the middle of the floor, I turned my back to him, threw my hands up to cup around his neck and began a heart-stopping grinding session. I grinned and look back at him as his hands began to move down my sides, gripping my waist. He started moving his own hips, grinding them against my swiveling behind. Less than a minute into the song I felt his growing arousal beneath his jeans. I released my hands from around his neck and turned to face him, continuing to allow my hips to move to the music. I felt his hands go around to cup my gyrating ass. I had to tamp down on the instinct to body slam him.

"Take me someplace quiet," I whispered once the song ended. To add understanding to what I was saying, I lowered his head to mine, and licked his lips, then moved my head to the side to nip at one of his earlobes.

"Mmm," he moaned, gripping my ass even tighter. "Let's go, Beautiful." He turned, pulling me off the dance floor and down the hallway he had been guarding. "Mannie, watch my spot for me for a little while," he told another guard that'd shown up from the other side of the room. Mannie grinned as he looked between me and Rodrigo. I kept my fake smile pasted on, but I really wanted to knee both men right where it hurts. Instead, I allowed Rodrigo to pull me down the hall, as he twisted doorknobs, testing to see which one was unlocked.

When we reached one that was unlocked he paused, and tossed me against the wall aggressively. A second later I felt his moist mouth cover mine and I fought hard to control my hands from clamping down on his carotid artery. Instead I tightened my fingers around his shoulders and turned my head slowly, to which he began kissing down my neck, leaving a trail of saliva from his sloppy kisses. When his hands moved down my ass and tried to make their way up my dress, I pulled back.

"Not out here out in the open, baby." I was proud of how coy I managed to sound.

"Okay, okay." He hurried and pushed the door open and stepped back a little to allow me to enter.

I entered the room and saw a huge leather couch and nightstand. I decided against sitting on the couch as my mind conjured up all kinds of thoughts of who'd been on it and what they've done.

"I've got protection. We're going to have fu--Oh shit!" Rodrigo yelled.

I slowly turned to see Liam with one hand pressed against Rodrigo's chest against the door, and the other held his piece to Rodrigo's face.

"What the fuck is this?" Rodrigo wondered, his eyes shifting from the glock, to Liam, to me.

I simply stood there with my arms folded.

"Bitch! You set me u-" his tirade was cut off as Liam stuck the barrel of his gun in Rodrigo's mouth.

"Show some Goddamn respect. She wasn't a bitch thirty seconds ago when you were feeling all over her ass." Liam's voice was dripping with disdain and I could tell he was close to losing it.

I suspected his ire was more a result of seeing Rodrigo touching and kissing on me more than the actual reason we were there.

"Li, he can't tell us anything if you kill him first," I reminded him, my tone flat and unbothered.

I watched as Liam contemplated for a few tense heartbeats before stepping back just a little, and removing the gun from Rodrigo's mouth.

"Mr. Bennett." Rodrigo's voice was one of complete surprise as he realized the man who just held a gun to his mouth was indeed the CEO of the company he was hired to do security for.

"You know me. Now, do you know why I'm here?" Li asked.

"I have no idea. All I know is this bi-" Again Rodrigo's angry diatribe directed at me was disrupted by Liam as he slammed the butt of his gun against Rodrigo's face. The crunch of breaking bones was evident, and the blood squirting was the dead giveaway that his nose was broken. "Ahhh, shit!" Rodrigo screamed, hunched over as he covers his nose.

"I told you to show some damn respect. Now, you've got blood on my sleeve." Liam's expression was deadpan. "Sit down!" Liam ordered Rodrigo.

I watched him slowly make his way over to the couch and sink down onto it still holding his nose and groaning. I pulled up one of the chairs from the other side of the room and sat directly in front of Rodrigo.

"I think it's broken," he whined.

"Oh, Jesus," I said. "I had my nose broken when I was twelve and didn't bitch as much as you are right now. Man up."

At that point, I was losing my patience and the way Liam was hovering over him told me that he was also.

Rodrigo gave me the eye and I knew he wanted to wrap his hands around my throat. I wished he would. I could tell he thought better of it when his gaze shifted to Liam and he cowered back on the couch.

"Look, we know you were there the night of Larry's accident. We also know you went to the junkyard to try gaining access to his car. I've also had some friends of mine do some digging. The week after Larry died you had $30,000 deposited into your account and another $10,000 a few weeks ago. That's a lot of money for someone who made $50,000 a year for the last three years. Care to explain?"

"I-I don't know what you're talking about." The widening of Rodrigo's eyes and sudden tapping of his foot was a dead giveaway that he was lying. As if I needed any more clues.

Behind me, Liam growled. He stepped around me to lunge at Rodrigo, but I placed my hand around his wrist.

I moved to pinch the bridge of his nose.

Rodrigo let out a loud wail of pain, but I remained unmoved.

"Rodrigo, as you can see here, Mr. Bennett has run out of patience. And so have I. You know something about Larry's death. Hell, maybe you were the one who set it up. Unless you start talking and I mean now, you'll be joining Larry in the afterlife." I was looking Rodrigo squarely in the eyes. I saw the very moment he decided to cooperate and I released his nose.

"Alright. It wasn't me," he said panting, "I didn't kill anybody. I just had someone come to me and ask me to do them a favor."

"Keep talking," Liam barked out when Rodrigo paused, wiping more blood from his nose.

"He said his name was John. He said all I had to do was make sure the cameras played on a loop for about five minutes while he went in the garage and that was it. I didn't think it was a big deal."

"Someone offered you $40,000 to have security cameras play on a loop in a place where employees park their vehicles for hours on end and you didn't think it was a big deal!?" The outrage in Liam's voice was apparent.

"I needed the money. I had some gambling debts…" Rodrigo's voice trailed off.

"Which they no doubt knew about," I said. "Finish the story. How did you end up at the junkyard?"

"I managed to play the video feed back and make it show on a loop for the time specified. Then when the money was deposited and I didn't hear anything back I didn't think anything of it. When I heard that guy died I got worried, but then the police ruled it an accident so I shrugged it off. A couple of months go by and nothing happens so I moved on. Except a few weeks ago this same guy, John, calls me on my cell, he says there's a problem and he needed me to go to the junk-yard. I told him I wasn't getting involved in any murder, but he told me I already was. That's when I got scared, so I did as he asked and went to the junkyard to look for some file that was in the car. When I was told I needed permission I backed off. I tried to go again a few days later and I was told someone had already come to look at the vehicle and released it to be crushed. Later that day I went to work and Ron asked me in for another interview. That's when I panicked and after that day I left town."

Liam turned his attention from Rodrigo to me, raising an eyebrow.

I looked at Rodrigo and note his gaze shifts downward to the left as he answered the questions. The tapping of his foot had ceased and even though he is in obvious pain, it's clear he's telling the truth. "He's being truthful," I told Liam.

Liam nodded and looked back at Rodrigo.

"Did John tell you who he worked for?" I questioned.

Rodrigo shook his head. "I asked him how he found me and he said his employer had ways, but he wouldn't reveal his name."

"How did he contact you?"

"The first time he approached me as I was getting in my car as I left the gym one day. The second time it was over the phone, although I never gave him my number."

I nodded. "We need access to your phone records. What did this 'John' look like?"

"Tall, kinda skinny, dark brown hair. Looked to be in his mid-forties."

"Alright, stand up," Liam ordered as he pulled Rodrigo out of his seat. "We need to make sure you don't run off anywhere."

"Wh-where are we going?"

"We're just gonna get you some medical attention for that nose and make sure you don't run off until we're able to track this John person down." Liam pulled Rodrigo towards the door. He opened it and there were already two of his own security staff waiting.

I followed as Liam gave them instructions on where to take Rodrigo for medical treatment and where to hold him afterwards. We left out the back door where there were two cars already waiting for us. Ron was the driver of the first car, while Mitch drove the second. Liam released Rodrigo to his security, and they took him to the awaiting car. I felt Liam's hand around my waist pulling me to the second car.

"We're going home." I felt his warm breath against the back of my neck and shivered at the earnestness in his voice.

* * *

CORAL

"I never left you."

Those words garnered my full attention. In spite of my desire to remain cold towards him, I took a chance and looked over at Liam on the other side of car. I noted the blur of the passing lights and street signs as we headed back to his home.

"Wh-what?" My voice had a slight tremble that I wasn't used to.

"I," he began slowly as his strong thigh muscles bulge beneath his Italian designer pants as he slid over closer to me.

I swallowed deeply, feeling like a deer caught in headlights as my eyes met his fierce gaze.

"Never left you," he repeated, this time pulling me to his side. "You're not often wrong, but you were wrong earlier today. I didn't leave. I…" he paused.

"You weren't there," I accused. "I woke up and you were gone. A few weeks later it's all over the news that you're engaged to be married. I sat in the…" I stopped myself from blurting out what I was going to say. "You weren't there," I said with finality and attempted to pull away.

Liam's grip around my waist tightened. "There are things you don't know. I'll tell you soon," I heard the sincerity in his voice and I wanted to believe it.

I couldn't get out a word before we pulled up to his driveway and soon enough to his front door. Liam continued to stare at me until the car made its final stop and Brian opened the door. Only then did our stare off end, but the warmth from Liam's gaze continued to emanate down to my very core. I wanted to believe him. I wanted to believe there was some deeper meaning behind why he left, but I was hesitant. There was always a part of me that believed I never fit in with Liam's world. I wasn't from a multigenerational family of wealth and privilege the same way he was. I didn't come from high society. I came from a world where fighting every day was a way of life, both inside and outside my home. Michele, the woman he married and who birthed his child was more on his level. She came from his world. Where the hell was I supposed to fit in all of that? That may have been the reason I waited until he told me first to confess that I was in love with him. That may have been the reason I left for years after he left. And I knew it was the reason I have yet to ask him outright why he left me five years ago. I didn't want to hear him confirm my suspicions that I just wasn't good enough to be the woman in his life. Not the one he married or had children with.

"Thank you, Brian. Make sure Rodrigo is well taken care of," I heard Liam say as we made our way to the front door.

I didn't even look back as Liam inserted the key and pushed the door open, while standing behind me. "I'm going to sleep in the guest room," I said, trying to put some distance between us. The words hadn't even fully left my mouth when my back was pushed up against the closed door, and Liam's arms bracketed either side of me.

His face was incredulous as he peered down at me. "Why the hell would you do that?"

"Li," I sighed out at a loss for words. I didn't have the energy to deny him.

"That isn't my room. It's *ours*," he emphasized the last word as if he was trying to tell me something important. I didn't have time to discern his meaning before his soft lips were pressed against mine. The logical part of my brain knew I should push him away and go to my own room to sleep. However, the feeling of Liam's lips as they made their way to that sensitive spot on my neck and his hand moving up under my dress, completely over rid any logical thinking for the night.

"Hssss," I hissed when his hand brushed over my bare labia.

"Another thing," he pulled back glaring at me.

I raised my eyebrow, angry as hell he'd stopped to freaking hold a conversation.

"Don't ever let another man put his hands or anything else on you." He dipped his head and bites my lower lip, sucking it into his mouth, licking it.

Something between a moan and sigh escaped my mouth at the same moment our tongues touched. I tasted a hint of rum and coke on Liam's lips and tongue, but instead of it making me nauseous like it did earlier, the taste, mixed with his natural taste, invigorated me. I kissed him back with same fervor and passion he was kissing me. His hands were now on my back, sliding the zipper of my dress down. I sent a silent prayer up thanking God for Laura's grandparents who had taken her for the weekend to make up for the previous weekend they had to cut short.

I felt Liam's strong hands at the back of my thighs, as he walked me backwards towards the stairs. Tonight I knew we wouldn't even make it to the bedroom before this first round was over. Liam broke away from my lips and stared down at me, those green eyes glittering with a fierce passion I'd only seen from him in moments like this. My mouth moistened and I could think of nothing else besides tasting him. Just as he began trying to pull down my dress I pulled back and turned him, pushing him down to the stairs, so his back was pressed against them. Kneeling in front of him I unbuttoned and unzipped his pants and belt buckle. I leaned up to his mouth, licked his lips and placed tiny kisses against his lips and face.

"Fuck."

That whispered curse sent a chill down my spine at the same time his cock jumped in my hand as I removed it from his boxers. I made eye contact with Liam as I licked my lips and the groan that escaped his mouth had the wetness in between my legs begin to slide down my inner thighs. I slowly drew my gaze down from Liam's eyes, down his broad body, and finally to his erect cock which stood at full attention in my hand. Even without an erection Liam was a sight to behold, but when fully erect his ten inches was glory.

"CeCe." The need in his voice was so apparent that I decided to finally put him out of his misery. I leaned down placing the tip of my tongue at the tip of his cockhead, swirling around the drop of precum that emerged. I moaned at the taste of him on my tongue right before I covered his entire head with my mouth. I go down until I felt him hit the back of my throat and there was still a few inches of him left exposed. I used both my mouth and hand to give his dick a massage.

"That's it, baby. Suck it," Li moaned and I picked up the pace, bobbing my head up and down on his length. I began to suck and slurp, making him hit the back of my throat with every down motion. I swirled my tongue around his stiffness, licking the thick vein on the underside on the way up. I smiled when I felt Liam's hand now in my hair, gripping my curls. I released his cock from my hand, still using my mouth to suck him off, while my hand trailed down to his balls and began massaging.

I felt Liam's cock grow even longer in my mouth and I knew with a few more strokes of my mouth he'd be coming. I began to ready myself for it, but was stopped. I peered up through my lashes and see Liam, pulling back from my mouth.

"I want to come inside you." His voice was full of strain.

I slowly allowed his cock to slip from my mouth with a loud "pop", and let him pull me up to straddle him. He pushed the sides of my dress all the way up, over my waist and up my arms, tossing it over the banister of the stairs. He maneuvered a little bit sliding his pants and boxers the rest of the way down to his ankles.

I braced my legs on his thighs and gripped the sides of his white button up, tearing them opened to feel the firm, rippling muscles of his stomach underneath my fingers. I allowed my hips to sink down onto his hardness and I tossed my head back moaning as he completely filled me up.

"Mmmm," we both moaned in unison. I paused looking down at him and our eyes locked. My pussy muscles clenched at the range of emotion I see in his eyes. In those dark green depths was possession, protectiveness, care, but most of all there was….love. Plain as day he lets me see it.

"Li," I sighed as I raised my hips and came down roughly, the smacking of my ass cheeks against his thighs echoed around the room. I rode Liam like he was a real life Texas cowboy. When I felt his fingers digging into my waist I stared down into his face. His heavily lidded gaze was tight with concentration. I pushed up again, squeezed my pussy muscles and slowly swiveled my hips as I lowered myself on his hard rod.

"Aw shit, ride that cock, CeCe."

I grew wetter at hearing the nickname only he called me and I quickened my movements. Sliding up and down his cock I reached back with one hand to grip his testicles and squeezed as I rode him. Liam let out a stream of curses and I knew he was only seconds away from coming, but so was I.

"I need you to come first," he insisted when he let go of my waist with one hand and used it to massage my clit.

"Aww," I moaned as I threw my head back again and allowed my orgasm to take over. I closed my eyes as he intensified the pressure on my exposed nub and I felt as if I was soaring. I lost my rhythm and gripped his arms to brace myself. At that time Liam took over and pushed himself up into me and soon enough I felt him erupt inside me as he grunted and moaned. His fingers dug into my waist pulling me down towards him. Our lips made contact among our hectic attempts to catch our breath.

"We'll finish this upstairs," Li said after pressing another kiss to my swollen lips.

I let out a huge sigh as I pushed up and he slipped from inside me, feeling the sense of loss. It didn't last long. After pulling his pants back up, Li swooped down, picking me up and carried me up the remaining steps and down the hall to our--I mean his bedroom.

* * *

Liam

"I don't like seeing other men touch you." Just thinking about that bastard's hands on Coral while they were dancing and again when he kissed her, had me wishing I'd done more than break his nose.

I felt Coral's smooth skin slide against mine as she rose from my chest to look up at me. We were lying in the bed, naked after another round of earth-shattering sex. Fuck that. What we did wasn't merely just sex. We made love. Yeah, I admit it, I was in love with this woman--always had been. When we fucked our bodies fully conveyed that love to one another. I knew she felt it too, but she held back.

Though the room is dim, I saw those hazel eyes as she rolled them, dismissing my earlier comment. "It was just a job. Don't get all crazy possessive," she said, waving her hand before resting her head back on my chest.

"It's way too late for that." My voice was deadpan as I looked down at her. I adjusted slightly to press a kiss to her forehead and then pulled her even closer to me.

"We haven't used protection."

My body stilled at those words. It was said low, almost tremulously. I wasn't easily shocked, but hearing the almost timid tone coming out of this woman's mouth was surprising.

"I'm not saying I'm pre--I'm not saying that. I'm just saying we haven't used condoms and I'm not on birth control," she admitted, looking up at me through those long lashes.

A stirring in my cock started both from her words and that look. I shrugged, "I haven't been with anyone since Laura's mother. Other than that..." I let those last words hang in the air so she gets my meaning.

She sat up fully staring down at me, eyebrows raised. "You haven't been with anyone else in the last five years?" She was clearly surprised. Her eyes watched me as I ran my hand through my hair, and sat up against the headboard.

I smiled when she stared at the bunching and rippling of my chest and stomach muscles as I shifted.

"No. Any other questions?"

"I don't make a habit of having sex without protection. You're the only person I've ever not used protection with."

I would have much rather preferred her stating she hadn't had sex with anyone else, but I already knew that wasn't the case.

"Not even Nate?" The question slipped out without me even thinking about it. *Shit.* By the way Coral's mouth turned down into a frown I knew that wasn't a good question to ask. But I couldn't control my jealousy. I'd lost five years with this woman due to shit beyond my control.

"Don't bring him up when we're sitting here naked in your bed."

I held up my hands in mock surrender. "Okay, okay. That was out of line," I said to appease her and calm her growing anger. That's the last thing I want right now. What I really want to do is flip her over, bury my cock deep inside her and shoot off another load, hopefully fertilizing an egg. Nothing would make me happier than Coral carrying my child.

She sighed. "We should start using condoms. I've been tested and

I'm clean. And as I said, I always use protection, but…" when she paused I made my move.

I pulled her face into mine and pressed a hard kiss to her lips. Using condoms wasn't going to happen so she should probably get comfortable with the fact she'd be carrying my kid soon, if she wasn't knocked up already. I could guarantee she'd be wearing my ring on her finger before she birthed a kid for me, but right then I was enjoying the feeling of my lips on hers. I pulled back, still holding her face between my hands. I looked into her eyes and saw the dazed, glossy look. I realized I'd effectively changed the topic. "You were saying?" I said in the cockiest tone I've ever used.

"Umm," was all she said.

I smirked.

"You're a bastard," she whispered, trying to hide her smile.

"You've always known that."

She pulled back slightly, and her eyes roll over my naked body. They paused once they reached my lower abdomen. Tentatively, she reached out and ran her fingers lightly across the rigid surface of the scar. "Does it still hurt?"

I shook my head. "Not for the last month." That was the truth. The injury had long since healed, but every now and again I'd felt slight pain or discomfort. It'd happened off and on for the last five years until recently. But since Coral had been back it hadn't bothered me. "Do you remember what you said when it happened?"

Her trailing fingers paused, still on my scar, but she kept her head lowered.

I placed my hand under her chin, not allowing her to avoid eye contact with me. "Do you remember what you said when it happened?" I asked again more demanding.

"Of course," she answered just above a whisper.

I could see her mind go back to that day in Iraq. We were stationed in Fallujah, and out for a sweep of the city looking for this one guy in particular. We all knew it was a fucking ridiculous mission. We were basically being used as bait to smoke out this insurgent who supposedly had ties to Al-Qaeda. We're in the middle of this densely populated city. Everyone was on high alert because just the week before an IED was set off killing one of our team. It was also the same explosion that caused Brian's injury and nearly killed him. Our squad got word that the guy we were looking for was hiding out in this shop. We made our way down to the two story building. We made entry and scoped out the rooms. Out of nowhere I saw someone running out of the corner of my eye. In a second I saw the target had a huge knife and was moving towards Coral. On instinct, I pushed her out of the way and took the plunge from the knife in my side. Shots rang out and all hell broke loose as I felt the warm, sticky blood as it oozed from my body. I remembered hearing Coral's, commanding voice, directing the rest of our team here and there, and then yelling my name. I grew more and more tired and just wanted to sleep, but the thread of fear I heard in Coral's voice wouldn't let me.

"I said, as long as I have you, I can get through anything." Her voice was soft, contemplative bringing me back to the present moment.

Those were the exact words she said as she begged me to not die as I was rushed to the Medevac. And just as it had done in that scorching desert, her words energized me. I moved fast, flipping her on her back and pressing her against the mattress with my body. "Did you mean it?" I questioned staring down into her shocked eyes.

"Liam..."

"*Did you mean it?*" I asked, bracketing her face between my hands, and brushing my leg against her inner thigh. She looked me directly in the eye and I hold my breath awaiting her answer.

"Of course."

I relaxed slightly at those words, but braced myself again for my next question. "Do you still mean it?"

Her eyelids lowered for a brief second before she looked at me again and nodded.

That wasn't good enough.

"Say it," I demanded.

"I can get through anything as long as I have you."

In the next second, Coral cried out as I drove my rock hard cock into her. I kept her face between my hands needing to keep the constant eye contact between us. I pumped my hips into her driving her body into the mattress. She wrapped her legs around my waist and her fingernails dug into my shoulders. Her cries and moans pushed me to drive deeper, harder until we were exploding together, staring in one another's eyes.

"We don't need condoms. You're going to be the mother of the rest of my children," I said hoarsely, as we both strove to catch our breaths. I didn't even pull out of her as we drifted off to sleep our bodies entwined.

CHAPTER 18

*C*oral

We don't need condoms. You're going to be the mother of the rest of my children.

Those damn words echoed around in my brain for the last four days. I wanted to say they angered me or completely turned me off, but I only lied when it was necessary for work. I stared across the table at Liam as he settled Laura into her chair for dinner and it made my heart swell at the little giggles he elicited from her. We'd been having family dinner every night. Most of the time, it was a dinner that Ms. Mary had prepared earlier in the day. Tonight, dinner was courtesy of yours truly. Yeah, I even found myself not hating cooking as much as I always had. Not when I was cooking for these two. *Who the hell had I become?* I asked myself as Liam set the plate of steamed broccoli, chicken parmesan and wild rice down in front of me. That'd became a part of this routine too. When I cooked, he cleaned and served.

I looked up to see those damn green eyes on me, a twinkle of laughter in them. He knew exactly what I was thinking and he was getting a kick out of it. To him, it was a foregone conclusion that this would be our life. I was not all the way there.

"After dinner can we make cookies?" Laura asked, breaking into my thoughts.

I felt my face soften from one of consternation to something gentler. *Love.* I realized as I looked across the table at this sweet little girl. I'd definitely fallen for this little one as well. I looked at Liam and again, the smirk on his face told me he's been reading me this entire time. I simply rolled my eyes at him before answering Laura.

"Only if you eat all your broccoli." Liam and I actually said at the same time.

Laura began to pout, but the rise of Liam's eyebrow quickly shut that down. "Okay," she grumbled and used her little plastic fork to eat her broccoli.

We spent the rest of dinner listening to Laura talk about her day in the animated way three years olds love to share. Afterwards, Liam collected the plates and cleaned up while Laura and I baked chocolate chip cookies. We had music playing in the background and I spun and twirled Laura around to the music, once we put the first batch in the oven. I saw Liam watching us out of the corner of my eye and I was...happy. Not just happy, but filled with joy, like this was where I belonged. And that feeling began to scare the shit out of me. Thankfully, before I could delve too much into my feelings of panic, the intercom buzzed alerting us that there was a visitor at the front gate. Liam threw the dish towel on the counter and told us to continue baking while he tended to whoever is at the door. I shrugged and was again distracted by the antics of the little one in front of me. We got lost in our own little world, giggling and playing as we watched the chocolate chips in the cookies slowly melt as they baked. I was so into the light-hearted feeling I didn't even hear Liam as he re-entered the kitchen with our guest. I only realized we were no longer by ourselves when the music stopped. I turned to see Liam standing there with a very stone faced Quincy. My stomach dropped.

Liam looked curiously between us two, frowning. I briefly contemplated what words were exchanged between the two men from the front door entrance to the kitchen. Quincy was probably the one person who was angrier at Liam than I was in the last five years.

"Hi!" Laura waved at Quincy, greeting him.

He looked down at her, studying her face, nodding in greeting. "Hello," he greeted her then looked back up at me.

"Quince," I said, clearing my throat. "What are you doing here?"

"That was my question," he retorted.

I sighed, knowing shit was about to get real.

"Liam, can you excuse Quincy and me?" I asked, moving towards the door, hoping Quincy would follow me and Liam wouldn't.

No such luck. Quincy remained still as a statue and Liam stepped in front of me eyeing me suspiciously.

"What's going on?" he asked.

I looked down at Laura, not wanting to make a scene in front of her. "Nothing, I just need to speak with my cousin. Alone," I said, stepping around him. "Quincy, follow me." My tone was clipped and I didn't look back as I exited the room. Eventually, I heard his footsteps following me as I entered the private dining room area. When he entered, I shut the sliding door, leaving only an inch or so of space open.

"Quincy what are you doing here?" I hissed at him.

His frown deepened. "That's a good ass question except you're directing it at the wrong person. Why the fu-" he paused when my eyebrow rose in warning. He knew not to talk to me like that. "Why are you here, Coral?"

"We were hired for a job," I stated, simply.

"We're hired for a lot of jobs and turn down jobs all the time. So again, why are you here?"

"How did you even know I was here? I thought you were in California."

"My case wrapped up early and I returned to Savannah to find out my little brother and cousin hiding the fact they took this case," he said.

Jabari was two years younger than Quincy, but hardly anyone's definition of little. Still at six-foot-two he is an inch shorter than Quincy's six-foot-three frame.

"We weren't hiding anything," I waved off his claim. "I expected to be finished with this case sooner."

"Oh, so that makes it alright. I can only guess what has held you up," he mocked.

I squinted at him, "Remember who you're talking to," my voice was low with a lethal undertone.

"I remember who I'm talking to. Do you? Do you remember being devastated after he left? Do you remember the nights I spent in the hospital with you afterwards?"

That reminder was like a slap in the face. It actually stung to think about that time.

"Now you're playing step mama to *his* kid with another woman. How is his wife by the way?"

"She's dead," the deep voice that reverberated around the room stunned both of us. "Died a month after giving birth," Liam offered.

"Sorry for your loss," Quincy spit out at Liam.

Liam looked between me and Quincy. "Why, were you in the hospital?"

I avoided Liam's gaze and shot Quincy a look with narrowed eyes, silently letting him know I was going to kick his ass for this. "Nothing," I said, waving off Liam's concern.

"Nothing?" Quincy's angry voice boomed around the room. "That's what we're calling it now? Nothing? Now, she's over here playing stepmother to your kid like she didn't lo—"

"Quincy!" I yelled, to stop him from saying anything else. If Liam was going to hear the rest it should be from my mouth.

Quincy glared at me, but remained silent.

I looked at Liam's perplexed facial expression. "Can you give us some privacy?" I asked Quince.

He remained staring at us for a few seconds before nodding and heading out the door.

"What the hell is going on? Were you sick?" Liam asked, concerned.

I let out a harsh breath. "No, I wasn't sick. I was pregnant."

The look on Liam's face told me a small gust of wind could have knocked him over. He obviously wasn't expecting that. "You had a baby?" he whispered.

I shook my head. "No," I sighed. "The pregnancy was ectopic."

He scrunched his eyebrows in confusion.

"It means the fetus started to grow in my fallopian tube instead of the uterus where it should have. The baby couldn't survive there. I didn't find out until I was nearly ten weeks and by then my fallopian tube had ruptured." I paused knowing this was the most difficult part. "I didn't know I was even pregnant until I began hemorrhaging and was in so much pain I passed out in my apartment. Quincy was the one who found me and got me to the hospital. I told him not to tell the rest of the family. I had to have emergency surgery to remove baby and save my ruptured fallopian tube."

Liam's face was a mask of confusion, anger, and guilt. His eyes traveled from mine down to my stomach and back up again. "You were carrying my baby?" His voice was just above a whisper.

"Yes, but…"

"And you almost died because of it. Meanwhile I went off and got fucking married."

The guilt and anger in his voice pulled at my heart strings. "Liam, it wasn't that bad," I lied, trying to console him. "Quincy was there for me."

"I should have been there!" His tone was sharp. "I should have been there." He slapped his chest harshly for emphasis. "I thought I was protecting you by leaving and I ended up hurting you more," he said out loud, but it was obvious he was talking to himself.

"Protecting me from what?" I questioned.

He stopped, realizing he'd said that out loud. We still had never addressed the reason he left in the first place.

"From shit you shouldn't have to worry about. I'm so sorry." He pulled me into his arms, stroking my back soothingly.

I was nearly pushed to tears remembering those days in the hospital realizing I had been carrying Liam's child and then lost it all in a matter of a few hours. Then finding out he was getting married while I was in the hospital.

"It was after that you went to work for the CIA?" he asked, pulling back to stare down at me.

I sighed and nodded. "I was being recruited heavily for months before then. I hadn't made any decisions. Then when you and I happened, I thought," I paused and shrugged. "Anyway, one night in the hospital I saw your engagement announcement on CNN. Three days later I was at The Farm."

"Fuck!" Li cursed, hearing how I ended up at the CIA's infamous training camp. He stepped back, hands tightly fisted, chest heaving as he tried to reign in his emotions. He began pacing back and forth and I gave him space to let everything sink in. I understand it's a lot of take in.

"Why aren't you still with them?" he suddenly asked.

I frowned in confusion. "What?"

"You were with the Agency barely, what? Three or four years?"

"Three and a half," I confirmed.

"What happened? Why did you leave?" He stopped directly in front of me.

I didn't feel like getting into all of that right now and thanks to a knock on the door I didn't have to.

Liam grunted at the interruption. "What?" he asked at the intruder.

"There's someone named Brian at the front gates. Says he had something important to share," Quincy answered, "And I still haven't fully explained why I'm here. It's about this case."

I immediately perked up at his last words. "What is it?"

"Jabari was able to get past the security passwords Larry had in place on the drive. You both should take a look at this," he explained.

"Let's go. You should let Brian in. He's been questioning Rodrigo and chasing down that John guy for the last few days," I reminded Li. I moved closer to the door to exit, and am stopped by Liam's strong grip around my wrist.

"This isn't over. You will tell me everything and soon." The command in his voice and the promise in his eyes actually turned me on. He didn't give me a chance to respond before he was leading me out the door.

I knew before this was all over that all of our secrets would be exposed.

CHAPTER 19

*L*iam

"We found him," Brian said excitedly, as I opened the door to the den.

My head was still spinning from finding out Coral was pregnant with my baby and that she nearly died as a result. I was distraught when Laura's mother died, not because I loved her. But I did care for her as a person and she was excited about being a mother. I had no idea what I would do if I had lost Coral. I'd felt like a shell of my former self for the last five years we were separated. If she had…I couldn't even let myself finish that thought.

"Liam, are you still with me?" Brian's voice broke through my musings.

"What did you find?" Coral's feminine, yet strong voice asked before I could pull it together.

I looked over at her and picked up on the fact that she was avoiding eye contact with me. Soon after Quincy arrived I called Laura's nanny to ask her to come watch Laura for the evening. I had a feeling this was going to be a long night just by the way Quincy was glaring at me since he first saw me. He and I had always had a friendly relationship, but I figured he was pissed at me for leaving Coral. I had no idea about the real reason. Shit, I was pissed as hell at myself, so I could understand where he was coming from. He'd always looked at Coral as a younger sister, although they only actually met after her father died and she and Stacey went to live with them. By then, Coral was already seventeen and a year from college.

I turned back to everyone in the den to refocus on the matter at hand. I was anxious to get this fucking case over with and solved. I wanted to know who killed Larry and why. Most of all, I wanted Coral out of danger. I'd known for a while there was something about this case that was of particular interest to her.

"Turned out, his name actually is John. John Walker," Brian continued. "I spent a few days and made a few calls to break into Rodrigo's phone. I traced the number Rodrigo said John called from back to a John Walker of Dallas, but currently lives in Austin."

Brian got my full attention when Austin was mentioned. I stared at Brian and I knew what he was going to say before he said it.

"He has ties to my father's office," I finished his statement for him.

Brian nodded. "He works as a low-level administrator, but get this. His salary is about a hundred thousand a year. That's a lot for a paper pusher don't you think?"

"Sure the hell is," Coral said.

"Do you have a picture of this John?" Quincy now asked.

"I do," Brian said pulling out a picture of the folder he'd been carrying.

We all looked at the picture and the guy did look familiar. I knew I'd seen him around my father's office when I visited.

"Yeah, it's the same guy," Quincy said.

Three pairs of eyes stared at him perplexed.

"Care to elaborate?" Coral requested.

"Jabari was able to get into the drive. That's the main reason I came. To deliver what he found. I printed it out also. On the drive was a picture of this same guy along with a lot of accounting records going years back. I took the time to go over the records to make sure what I found." He stopped to pull out the picture and sure enough it was the same person. Then he pulled out page after page of financial data from Bennett Industries. All of these records, however, were from nearly two decades ago. Long before I took over as CEO.

"What is this?" I asked, looking over the unfamiliar records.

"These are the real financial records of your company. Turns out, during the late nineties during the oil crisis, your father made a deal with the devil."

"My father is the devil," I interrupted Quincy.

He simply nodded and continued. "You may be right about that. He got in with some unscrupulous men who ran guns, girls and drugs to bail his company out. Of course, they used shell companies to make it look as if everything was above board. Since then, your father was helping to fund that criminal enterprise. It looks like it's been with the assistance of John here."

"Did you say drugs, guns and girls?" Coral asked. Her voice was low and deadly.

"Yup. The governor of Texas has been aiding in funding an international sex, gun and drug ring. Of course, that side of the world doesn't know who he is. They all know him as the Ghost because he's virtually invisible."

"Oh. My. God." Coral gasped.

* * *

CORAL

Holy shit! Was the only coherent thought my brain could form with the realization that Liam's father was Ghost. The bastard who killed my team. But why? This didn't make any sense.

"What is it?" Liam's strong voice pulled me out of my thoughts.

I stared at him. "Your father tried to kill me."

"What?!" yelled Liam, Quincy and Brian all at once.

I looked between the three of them. "You asked why I left the Agency," I began. "Almost two years ago, I was on an assignment in Colombia. We were tracking an international terrorist known for running drugs, guns and girls into the U.S. We had no idea what he looked like. There was no picture of him. Not even a real name. My team gets a tip that someone high up in the guy's network was staying in this little pueblo outside of Bogota. We set up a meet with the person who gave us the tip, but something was nagging at me. It didn't feel right. I didn't read any dishonesty from the guy who gave us the tip, but still it just wasn't right. So, I set up another meet with a previous contact I trusted—well trusted as much as possible in that world. Anyway, I get ready for that meet and told Sheila and Don, my team, not to do anything until I got back. I told them not to make a move." I paused, overwhelmed by the guilt.

"What happened?" Liam's sincere voice wrapped around me, blanketing me in security.

"They didn't listen. Sheila was young, and had been recruited right out of undergrad. She was less than a year out of The Farm. She was smart, capable, and she had a great career ahead of her, but she was ambitious. Wanted to prove to me that she could handle the mission. Don was loyal. He'd never let anyone of us walk into danger alone, so when Sheila opted to keep the meet, he went with her. It was a set up. There was a bomb set to a timer in the bar where the meeting was. Sheila and Don never saw it coming." I paused again.

"You never told me any of this," Quincy stated almost accusingly.

I turned to him. "I never told anyone. After the bombing, I was put on desk duty while an investigation took place. It looked suspicious that my team was killed and I made it out unscathed. I got that. But I fought hard to prove that I had nothing to do with it and was just as dead set on finding out who was behind it. I was cleared, but it still felt like someone above me was pulling strings. The assignments I was given felt more risky, little intel and not enough back up. I started to believe the bombing was an inside job so I resigned. I've been investigating on my own ever since. A few months ago I was led to a guy who ran girls up through Mexico. He told me the name I was looking for was Ghost." I saw Li's eyes widen in shock. "For whatever reason this Ghost had it in for me. A month later, Jeremy winds up in Savannah saying an employee of yours was killed, but he left a message saying something about a Ghost being behind suspicious financial activity some years back in Bennett Industries." I looked

Liam in the eye. "I came for two reasons. One, you were in danger and two, I need to get the bastard who killed my team. Sheila and Don should still be here. Don had a wife and kids. They deserve justice."

"He fucking went through with it," Liam's said, his voice just above a whisper.

My brows crinkled in confusion. "What?"

Li remains silent for a few seconds.

"I told you I didn't leave because I wanted to. The night I left I got a call from my father. I never told him about us or that I was planning on proposing to you. Somehow he found out. He woke me in the middle of the night, telling me he wouldn't allow this to happen. Of course, I told him to go fuck himself. I couldn't care less about being kicked out of his will or even not being allowed to take over Bennett Industries. I would have given it all up for you."

His words sent a shiver down my spine.

"He knew that though. When his threatening to cut me off didn't work, he made real threats. He threatened your life. Not just yours, but your family. He knew everything. Where you lived, where Stacey lived, Jabari, Quincy, your aunt and uncle. He even knew about Tasha. He recited all their addresses and said he had guys following them ready to do whatever at his word. I knew they weren't idle threats so I agreed. He'd been pressuring me for years to marry Michele and take over Bennett Industries as his sole heir. Her father had important political ties that helped him win the election, and he believed she was better for the image of a CEO than you," he stated looking at me. "I left, cutting off all contact and married who he wanted me to, to keep you safe. I've spent the last five years trying to gather information on him to take him down. Larry was originally a forensic accountant. That's why I hired him a year after I took over Bennett Industries. He died because of this."

"Did anyone else know why you hired him?" Quincy asked.

"Only Jeremy and he wouldn't tell anyone."

I knew Jeremy wouldn't go against Liam. He owed Liam too much.

"You have the proof that my father is the ringleader of all this? It needs to be tangible so I can take it to the right people to have that bastard locked up for good."

Quincy nodded, fanning out the papers on the table in the room. "All the evidence is here."

We spent the next hour poring over the financial records that it must have taken Larry years to track down and compile. We discovered the man Li's father originally borrowed money from was the son of a crime family out of New York that originated down in Colombia. He lent the company almost twenty million dollars. With that exchange, Liam's father began helping him clean the money from his criminal activities. Once the son died, it looked like Liam's father took over and began running drugs, guns and worst of all, girls. He didn't run for low level criminals either. Records showed he had connections in very high offices around the country, including in the CIA. No wonder he was able to nearly kill me.

"Your op in Bogota was getting close to discovering the truth," Quincy said as we examined the records showing his Colombian connection. "It's why he tried to take you out."

"No, not the only reason," Liam interjected, looking down at me. "He told me he'd leave you alone if I did his bidding. Took over Bennett Industries while he ran for and became governor. I complied, but I'm sure he already knew I never intended to stick with that plan. I've been making moves to uproot him for years. I think he suspected as much."

"You two have been playing chess," I said.

Li nodded. "Trying to kill you was his final checkmate, or so he thought."

The look in Li's eyes was deadly.

"It's time to pay my father a visit."

"I'm not staying here," I informed him.

"No one is. I don't want you out of my sight."

"Wait," I said turning to Quincy. "I need you to do me a huge favor."

"I'll get Jabari to cover Stacey for protection and inform her and

Andre of what's going on," he said knowing that my sister's safety in all this would be at the forefront of my mind.

"No, I can do that," I countered." I need you to go to Vermont for me."

"What the hell is in Vermont?"

"Tasha. I don't have time to explain. I'll just say she's a friend, a close friend and I won't let anything happen to her. Li said his father knew about her so he could try to get to her too. Here's her address," I began writing down her Vermont address. "I can arrange for a private plane and car to take you to her."

He stared at me for a few seconds. Whatever he saw in my eyes must have let him know I was serious. He agreed and took the address, pulling out his phone to arrange the flight and car service.

I needed to make a call to Tasha first. She didn't take well to new people and I knew she'd be frightened by Quincy's brooding, burly self, approaching her. Li's hand on my arms stopped me. He pulled me to the side and his hands gripped my waist, tightly. He put his forehead against mine. I could tell he was blaming himself for all this. The anguish on his face made me want to console him. I reached up and stroke his cheek.

"I should have protected you better. I thought I was doing the right thing. I'd do anything to protect you. He will pay for your team, for Larry and for keeping me from you when you needed me most," he said, as his hand slid down covering my womb. "I'll spend the rest of our lives making it up to you," he promised, pressing a kiss to my forehead.

I smiled up at him, and pressed a kiss to his soft lips. "I just might let you."

CHAPTER 20

*L*iam

I stared down at a sleeping Coral. We were thirty thou-sand feet in the air on the plane towards Austin. I could think of nothing more than to finally have this shit over with, getting my father out of the way and finally having this woman to myself. I knew what we were about to reveal was going to set off a shit storm around the nation. The governor of a major political state had also been running an international crime ring for more than a decade. The same governor who has very publicly discussed the possibility of entering the run for President. Yeah, there was about to be some shit. But none of that concerned me. What I was most concerned about was keeping this woman lying in the bed beside me out of harm's way. She and my daughter were the most important things to me in this world. If anything were to happen to either one of them I'd lose my fucking mind.

"You going to keep staring at me this whole flight?" she asked, her eyes still closed.

"I thought you were asleep." I couldn't help smiling as she slowly opened her eyes.

"The only place I can actually sleep is your house," she said looking around the private jet's small bedroom.

Laura was out in the main cabin, sleeping next to Brian. Ron and the rest of my security were out there as well. I couldn't leave the two most important people in my life behind.

"*Our home*," I corrected her last statement.

Her eyes widened and she just stared at me.

I decided it was time to tell her everything. "Don't look so shocked. Why do you think you had that reaction the first time you saw the house?"

She looked down trying to recall the first time I brought her home after her hotel room was broken into. She looked back up at me, a surprised, questioning look on her face.

I nodded answering her yet-to-be-asked question. "You remember that night we stayed up talking about the house of our dreams?"

She nodded.

There were many nights we stayed up talking about what we would do when we got home after our tour. It helped pass the time out in the desert. One night we started talking about our dream homes. Coral mentioned that her dream home had lots of huge windows. Growing up in the projects there were few windows, and the ones that existed were covered by steel bars to prevent falls. She said she'd want it outside of a city so there'd be no constant blaring from sirens or other typical city noise. I always carried that with me and made sure the home I built for us had huge windows and lots of open space.

"It's *our* home. Always has been. I built it for us."

She sat up staring at me, silently.

I reached out to caress her cheek with my hand. I was always amazed at how soft her skin was. Her career and demeanor gave her a hard edge. But the softness of her skin reminded me of the different layers beneath the surface. The layers she rarely allowed anyone else to see.

"Why would you do that?" she asked almost timidly.

"You have to know by now that I had every intention of coming back for you. I never left because I wanted to. I left to keep you safe. Seems I didn't do such a great job of that," I admitted, frowning. "But, you've always belonged to me. Even when you didn't know it."

She lowered her head for a second and looked up at me smirking. "Is that why you went to visit Nate a few weeks ago?"

My eyes narrowed. If that bastard went crying to her about my little visit the tiny amount of respect I had for him was going right out the window.

"No, he didn't tell me," Coral continued. "He stopped calling right around the time you returned from your trip and I overheard your driver saying you left a pair of sunglasses in the backseat after your trip to D.C. I put two and two together."

I chuckled. Of course, she would figure it out.

"You know a relationship normally works when the couple mutually decides to be together," she joked.

I took her hand in between both my hands. "Sweetheart, when the hell has anything between us ever been normal?" I asked, right before covering her lips with mine.

It was a true statement. For all intents and purposes, Coral and I should have never met. She was a girl from one of the toughest communities in New York City, and I'm a Texas good 'ol boy, born with a silver spoon in my mouth. Some would say we were an unlikely pair, but those people wouldn't know the truth, which is that this woman saved me. She taught me there was life and humanity beyond the selfish world I was raised in. I was a better man, father, and I would be a better husband all because of her. And I intended on showing her that right now.

"Mmm," she moaned as I place kisses down her jawline and lick the spot just below her ear.

"Shhh, CeCe. We're going to have to be quiet this go 'round," I said reminding her we're not alone on this jet.

When she whispered my name in that sexy lilt, my cock jumped in my pants and I knew I needed to be inside her soon. I pushed her down against the mattress and unbuttoned and pulled her jeans down before quickly doing the same to my own clothing.

"Damn, CeCe, you're soaking wet," I crooned in her ear, touching her wetness with my fingers.

"Only for you, Li."

Those words had an instant impact on my cock, making me painfully hard. I pulled Coral's legs up to my waist and pushed all of myself into her in one fell swoop. I didn't immediately begin pounding her like my rock hard dick was telling me to. Instead I paused, staring down into the only face I ever wanted to see in this position again. "Can you still have kids?" I asked the question that'd been lingering in my mind since she revealed that she lost our child.

"Wh-what?" she panted and it was the sexiest fucking sound ever.

"Can you still have kids?" I asked again, beginning to thrust my hips.

She nodded.

"And it's not a health risk?"

"No....the doctors said I should...be able to...carry and have...a healthy pregnancy and birth in...the future." She panted and moaned with every down stroke of mine.

"Good. Cuz we're making a baby. Again." With those words I picked up my pace and thrusted my unyielding cock into her with every bit of strength of I had. When her moans got a little too loud, I fused our mouths together. I reached down with both my hands, propping her waist up, allowing me to go even deeper. Coral gripped my shoulders tightly and kissed me back with the same amount of passion.

Goddamn I love this woman. That was the only coherent thought running through my head as we fucked each other's brains out as quietly as possible. I felt her wetness grow and her pussy muscles tightened around my cock and I knew she is coming. She ripped her lips from mine, turned her head and biting my upper arm to keep from yelling out. The pain mixed with her tight, clutching pussy shattered me and I lowered my head into the crook of her neck, shouting my release. My thrusting hips continued pumping ensuring every last drop of my seed made its way into her canal.

"As soon as this is all over," I said low in her ear, as we both struggled to catch our breath, "I'm officially making you mine."

She simply stared at me.

I pressed my lips to the corner of her mouth, and turned us so we're both on our sides, still facing one another. Our bodies still joined. Minutes later our pilot alerted us we were making our final descent into Austin. Good. I was ready for this final checkmate against my father and to lay claim on my queen.

CHAPTER 21

*C*oral

I was nervous. This was new for me because I didn't get nervous in these situations. Angry? Yes. Perturbed when things didn't go my way? Possibly. But not nervous. I knew it was because the stakes were personal this time. I'd found out the real reason Li left and it only made me love him that much more. I wanted to be his, but I didn't know if I was ready. I looked over at Laura who was drawing on the table set up in this huge hotel suite we were staying in. We'd been huddled up for hours with the FBI, turning over page after page of evidence against Liam's father. It was difficult to comprehend that a U.S. governor would betray his own country like this for money, and most of all, power. But, I'd seen people do a lot to get and maintain power. I was hardly shocked by it anymore.

The head of San Antonio's FBI was livid. "I can't believe this!" he yelled. Although it had taken some maneuvering, we were actually able to get him here. Clearly, he was dumbfounded by the information we'd presented to him. "He's been doing this right under our noses. And from the looks of it, he's not alone. This goes all the way up to members in the Senate and House of Representatives. I'll need to call the Director immediately, and get our men in place."

"The Director had already been contacted," Liam said. "The Director of the FBI was one of my first phone calls when we got the information back in Dallas. I've been in contact with him for a while now trying to get an angle on my father. He is actually flying out as we speak. We're going to make some phone calls and take a trip to visit dear old dad. I expect you to have your men in place," Li said before turning back to the papers on the table.

Leave it to Liam to give orders to an FBI field office director like it was his job.

Everyone began scrambling to come up with a plan to execute. We already knew the press was going to have a field day with this. Not to mention the type of international trouble this would cause. I stepped away to take a break from it all. My job would be to remain here with Laura and let the men go off and do their thing. For once, I was okay with not being the ringleader of this mission. I gazed out the window, watching the Austin skyline and remembering the first time I did this back in Dallas. It felt like so long ago, but it was only about a month and a half. I began to wonder what life after this would be like. I'd been ripping and running for so long trying to escape my demons, some real, some made up, that I never took the time to ponder a life outside of working to save others. Could I see myself married and as a mom? Do I even want that?

"What are you thinking about?" The deep voice penetrated my thoughts and warmed my entire body like a favorite blanket, as Liam's strong arms enveloped me from behind.

"You. Us. All of this," I answered honestly.

"Stop wondering," he commanded, spinning me around to face him. "You and I were always meant to be here. From day one it's been me and you. Bullshit got in the way of that, but I won't let anything else come between us." His voice was so full of certainty I couldn't help but trust it. This was the only man I'd ever felt safe enough to feel this way with.

I looked up into his emerald green eyes and reached up pushing a dark blond lock of hair away from his handsome face. "I love you, Li."

"'Bout damn time," he said, grinning like I just served him the world on a platter. "I love you, CeCe. Always have. Always will."

I smirked. "I'm holding you to that. Bring your ass back here in one piece," I told him.

"Will do, Sergeant Coleman." He mock saluted me and then gripped my ass firmly right before he delivered another soul stealing kiss.

"Take care of our Princess," he said after pulling back.

I turned my head looking over at Laura who was now playing with a doll on the couch. I smiled at her innocence. "With everything I have."

"I'm leaving Ron here to watch the both of you." He held his hand up when I frowned. "It would make me feel better knowing someone is watching out for the both of you."

"I will watch out for the both of us," I narrowed my eyes at him.

"And Ron will as well." He kissed the tip of my nose. I relented only because that was not the time to argue. Soon, Liam would be responsible for sending his father to jail for a very long time, but also causing a huge media storm and turning his mother's life upside down and causing a media storm.

"Alright. Fine," I agreed.

"You should start thinking about what wedding dress you want to wear on our big day," he said.

I rolled my eyes.

"Or, you could wear jeans. Either way, we'll need to set a date."

"Shouldn't you be thinking about the fact you're about to send your father to jail?" I asked.

"I can do both. Anyway, we'll be back soon enough and this will be all over. Have the dress chosen by the time I get back." He gave me one last kiss before going over to Laura. I grinned widely when she began giggling from his tickles. I watched them for a few minutes until I noticed movement out of the corner of my eye. Ron was watching Li and Laura. I chill went down my spine, but I didn't have time to analyze it before my phone vibrated in my pocket. It was Tasha. I called her as soon as Quincy left the house to let her know he was on his way. I sent a picture so she knew exactly who he was. He called as soon as he arrived to confirm. I still haven't told Tasha exactly what's going on and of course, she was antsy.

"Hey Tash," I answered.

"Now, can you tell me what's going on?" She sounded exasperated and a little nervous.

"Okay. It's like this…"

I told her all of what I can for now. I wanted to ease her fears and let her know she could trust Quincy with her life, but I didn't want to scare her. I also sent Jabari to Atlanta and told him to take my Aunt and Uncle, to make sure they were all together and safe. Now, it was a waiting game. I watched as the FBI agents, Li's security, Brian, and Liam head out the door. He gave me one last look back and reassuring nod before closing the door behind him.

I looked at my phone and saw that it was almost ten a.m. But given that we'd been up for hours it felt like so much later. Yet, I was much too anxious to feel tired. I knew whatever happened today would determine the course of the rest of my life. I sighed and headed towards the living room couch to play with Laura.

* * *

Liam

I was feeling anxious. Not the nervous or scared type of anxious, but the "I'm ready to get this shit over with," anxious. I'd been waiting for this moment for far too long. Yes, I was here to take down my own father. The man who taught me to play chess. Who was a bastard my entire childhood unless we were out in public. I'd waited years to put the right pieces in place to take this man down. I used the game he taught me to maneuver around him and take him down.

As we entered the gates to the Governor's mansion I felt my fingers twitch. When the FBI field director requested I leave my gun in my vehicle, I glared at him for nearly a full minute before conceding. It was likely for the best. No telling what I might've done if my father started spouting off his bullshit, especially if he said anything about Coral. My father and I had spent very little time in the same room in the last five years for a good reason. He'd only met my daughter once. Of course, for the media it was spun as the Bennett family leading very busy lives, but the truth was I'm not all that sure I could have resisted putting my fingers around his throat and squeezing as the life flees his body. Just thinking about it sent a jolt of energy through my body. I cracked my knuckles.

"You're right. I don't need my gun," I smiled devilishly at the field director.

His eyes lowered watching as I cracked my knuckles. "There's no need for this to get physical either," he said.

I simply stared, agreeing to nothing. "Let's go," I motioned my security. I knew the director was probably perturbed by my taking the lead, but he'd just have to suck it up. I had waited too long for this.

We headed up the pathway to the front entrance of the mansion. I looked up to see the plantation style, crisp white building with six huge columns along the front entrance. Hanging from two of the columns was an American flag and the Texas state flag. I shook my head thinking of how my good for nothing father betrayed both of those flags. The flags I'd risked my life fighting for overseas. He'd betrayed me in more ways than one.

The security guard who opens the door looks surprised to see me heading this group of men. "Mr. Bennett."

"Sir, we're with the FBI," the director announced, holding up his credentials.

I didn't wait for any instructions. I knew exactly where my father was. I moved down the long hall towards the main office. My father's secretary looked up surprised, prepared to speak. I held my hand up, cutting her off, then snatched the door to his office open; unfortunately, I was granted a view of my father's bare ass as he thrust in and out of some brunette he had bent over his desk.

"I guess we can add this to the already long list of adulterous behavior when mom files for divorce," I stated casually, folding my arms across my chest.

"Goddammit!"

"Oh, my God!" My father and the woman both yelled at the same time. The girl shrieked and tried to cover her face, but I still recognized her. She was an intern in his office.

"Typical," I chuckled and shook my head.

"What the hell is going on?!" my father bellowed when he noticed that I was with an army of men behind me. The way he hurriedly tried to stuff himself back into his pants was comical. The two were a tangle of arms and legs trying to affix their clothing as five pairs of eyes watched them.

"Liam what the hell is this about?!" he demanded.

"Young lady, you probably want to leave immediately and go home and update your resume," I said looking squarely at the red-faced young woman, ignoring my father. This angered him even more.

"You don't get to fire my damn staff! I don't know what you think you saw, but-"

I held up my hand, cutting him off. "She'll need a new job because by the time you leave this office, you'll be stripped of the position of Governor. You can leave now," I said sternly to the girl, whose head was lowered.

Without any words she scurried out of office, shamefaced.

"Bert, what are you doing here?!" My father looked over my shoulder and saw the field director standing there. As governor, my father had met all the field directors in the state on numerous occasions.

"How could you, Richard?" Disappointment was evident in his voice.

"Look, you know how these young girls are. They come to work in these tight skirts-"

"Shut up!" I yelled. I was sick of hearing his shit. "No one gives a fuck who you fuck, least of all me. Hell, your wife doesn't even care as long as it's not her. But betraying your state, your country while shaking hands with your constituents and holding babies for the cameras? All this time you were funneling poison to the most vulnerable. The ones you were supposed to protect." I took a menacing step closer. My fingers twitched with anticipation as my father puffed up his chest trying to intimidate me the way he did when I was a child.

"I have no idea what you're talking about."

He was lying. I could see it clear as day in those green eyes so much like mine. "This," I snatched the file out of the director's hands and tossed it at him. Papers fly everywhere. "Take a fucking look." I pointed at the papers scattered on the hardwood floor.

Ever prideful, he refused to bend down to pick the papers up. Instead, he looked down at them trying to read them. When he reached the first picture of him with a well-known drug runner out of South America his facade slipped a little. His eyes moved to the next picture of a brothel just outside of Texas, on the Mexican side of the border where he kept many of the girls that were trafficked and his face whitened. As the cold, hard reality that his time had finally come he visibly deflated. For some reason that pissed me off even more.

"You know you caused your own demise," I said, menacingly, taking another step closer, right on the very papers he was looking at. I got directly in his face. "The moment you threatened my woman's life you started the countdown to this moment."

"I was doing you a favor!" he shouted. "That girl is not right for you. I groomed you to lead Bennett Industries. To do what needs to be done when times get tough. I taught you to make the hard decisions to get ahead. So what I had to get my hands dirty to get where I am. So what! You meet some girl in college and all of a sudden you care about the little man and being a fucking do-gooder. On top of that you hire that bastard nephew of mine! That gets you nothing in this world. Fuck that little bitch. I should have killed her in Colombia when I-"His diatribe was cut off when my hand began s crushing his wind-pipe. "L-Li-," he struggled trying to remove my lethal grip from his throat.

"Liam!" I heard and felt the director yelling and pulling me to release my father, but all I kept hearing are his threats on her life.

Suddenly an image of Coral and Laura giggling together the night before as they made cookies penetrated my mind. I pulled myself back from the edge. "I could kill you right now," I threatened. "But death would be too easy for you. You deserve to live and watch your entire life crumble before you. Then you deserve to spend your last breaths locked in a six by eight foot cell." I pushed him away, nearly causing him to fall to the floor, but his fall was stopped by the FBI agents on either side of him.

I heard him coughing and wheezing as I made my exit. I had no need to lay eyes on him any longer. I didn't even look back to see if Brian or any of my security team was following me. I took my first deep breath and began to let myself feel free for the first time in five years. The only thing I wanted to do is get back to my ladies. Before I could get too excited the hairs on the back of my neck stood up as I heard the almost maniacal laughter of my father behind me. He was being lead escorted by FBI agents on either side of him as his hands are cuffed behind his back, and yet he is laughing. The pit in my stomach grew.

He was looking directly at me. "You think this is over?" he gloated.

I narrowed my eyes but didn't say anything.

"I never fully trusted you either. You're not the only one who had spies." His eyes darted around looking at everyone that's come with me. "I see you didn't bring that little bitch with you. You should have."

I took long strides towards him and gripped him by the front of his shirt. "What the fuck are you talking about?!" I snarled.

"How did you think I knew about you and her? How you planned to propose? You never would have told me that. How did you think I knew about what hotel room to send my men to?"

I paused for a heartbeat. I stared into his eyes and the answer became apparent. "Shit!" I turned and began running towards the door. "We need to get to Coral and Laura now!" I yelled to the men with me.

CHAPTER 22

Coral

"Hey, stranger. I guess I was right." Nate's tone was light, but I could hear a bit of melancholy in it.

"Right about what?"

"That you lied when you said you weren't the marrying kind."

"I didn't lie," I defended myself.

"Not to me. You were lying to yourself. You weren't the marrying kind for me, but for him."

I ran my hand through my short curls. This was not why I called Nate. I peeked over at the opened bedroom door and noticed Laura stirring awake from her nap. "I'm not married," I told Nate.

"Not yet, but if the way your man showed up to my office a few weeks ago is any indication he's definitely told you, you're getting married. And you either said yes, or didn't outright refuse, which is just as good as a yes. You had no problem telling me you didn't even want a real relationship."

I really hated when people could read me so easily. I didn't say anything because there was nothing to be said.

"It's all good. You never lied or lead me on. You told me your stance; I just wished it could be different. I had a thing for you ever since the first time I laid eyes on you. But the truth is, everyone knew it was you and Liam from the get go. Some of the guys even had bets to see how long it would take you both to make it official. I never participated 'cause they'd secretly pissed me off, though I wouldn't show it," He chuckled.

"Oh yeah," I asked, absentmindedly, staring across the room at Laura and Ron.

"But you know who would get really pissed about those bets?"

"Who?"

"Ron. I remember he'd damn near blown a gasket if anyone around mentioned you and Liam. I see he's part of Liam's security team now."

For some reason Nate's words send a prickly feeling down my spine. The same feeling I'd gotten earlier as I spotted Ron eyeing Laura and Liam. Never one to ignore my gut instincts I stored that information for later use.

"So, you obviously didn't call to tell me you were ready to give us a shot, so what's up?"

Blinking a few times to remember the initial purpose of my call, I began, "Listen, some shit is about to go down. And as a Senator on the Committee on Homeland Security it's gonna land right in your lap. I just wanted to give you a heads up."

"Does this have to do with Liam's father?"

"What about Li's father? You know something?" I asked trying not to give away any details, but wanting to find out what Nate knew.

"I don't have anything concrete, but there have been low whispers about him for a while now. I really hope your boy is clean."

"My *boy* is fine," I iterated, defensively, knowing he was referring to Liam. I knew my man had nothing to do with the illegal dealings his father participated in.

"He better be. I refuse to lose to an international terrorist."

"You didn't lose, Nate. You and I just..."

"We weren't meant to be. I can take a hint, finally. Listen, thanks for the heads up. I have go."

"Bye." I hung up quickly not wanting to prolong that awkward conversation any more than he did. I looked back over at Laura and

Ron and that same prickly feeling returned. Laura was sitting on the floor coloring and singing to herself. It was adorable, but for most of the morning, I'd noticed anytime Ron tried to interact with her, she'd shy away from him. This wouldn't catch my attention too much any other time, but Laura wasn't really the shy type, and Ron had worked with Li for years. She should be used to his presence by now. My gut was telling me something was off, and I was pretty sure young Laura's natural instinct had picked up on it as well. Kids were often better than most adults at reading people. When they were this young, they hadn't become weighed down by societal expectations or pressures to be nice or polite, especially young girls. If they didn't like someone it was apparent. What my eyes were seeing was that Laura, for whatever reason, was no fan of Ron's.

"Hey Laura, do you have to go potty?" I questioned jovially making my way over to her.

She gave me a contemplative look and shook her head. "No."

"How about you try anyway? Then you can finish coloring in the bedroom." I began picking up her crayons and coloring books and took her hand to lead her in the bedroom towards the bathroom. "We may be in here a little while," I tossed over my shoulder to Ron who was now giving me a curious look. I didn't waste time trying to figure him out. As casual looking as possible, I led Laura into the bedroom, shutting the door behind us. Unfortunately, there was no lock.

"Sweetie, just see if you need to use the bathroom, okay?" I pleasantly smiled down at Laura so she didn't pick up on anything. I sighed in relief a little when she headed towards the bathroom with no more questioning. I sent a text to Jeremy, praying he gets back quickly.

Hey, who knew what room I was in, in the hotel?

Only me, Liam, his top security. That's it.

Ron? I responded immediately.

Yeah. Him

The message was short, as if he is having a realization as his fingers were typing.

You don't think...

I do. I responded.

Where are you?

In the damn hotel room with him and Laura. I'll handle it. I finished before stuffing the phone back in my pocket. I already know Jeremy was on the phone dialing Li's number.

"I finished. I did a little tinkle," Laura emerged from the bathroom giggling.

"Did you wash your hands? Go back and wash them," I pointed to the bathroom, trying to buy a little more time. When she turned back I went straight to my overnight bag and pulled out my glock and made sure it was loaded. I barely slipped the gun behind my back and into the waistband of my jeans before Laura was back. "Hey you, how about we go out and get you, me, and daddy some ice cream?"

Laura's eyes instantaneously lit up at the mention of a beloved treat. "With sprinkles?"

"Sure thing." I grabbed her hand and headed towards bedroom door. As soon as I opened the door, Ron was standing right there. I stared in his brown eyes and see it: the cold, the hatred.

"Going somewhere?" On the surface his voice was harmless enough, but I detected even the most minute intonations and inflections. His were telling me something a lot more sinister.

"We're going to get ice cream," I said taking a step to move past him, shielding Laura with my body, but he moved with me.

"I doubt that's going to happen," he gritted out.

I felt something hard pressing into my lower abdomen and I didn't have to look down to know it was the business end of gun. I gripped Laura's hand tighter and pushed her body even further behind me. I stared Ron dead in his eyes and smiled. "You've been waiting for a while to do this, haven't you?"

"Yup."

"How's it feel?" My own voice had taken on a lethal tone. He was too stupid and emotional to realize it, but he was no longer looking at Coral. The Scorpion had just made its appearance.

He actually had the audacity to smile. "Feels pretty good."

Stupid. "Not that. I mean, how's it feel to know you're about to take your last breath?" I asked, pressing myself even closer into him.

For less than a tenth of a second his face was a mask of perplexity, but before he could even comprehend my last statement, I'd gripped his wrist, pushing his hand up towards the ceiling, and elbowing him in the ribs.

Boom.

The gun went off, one nine millimeter bullet crashing into the ceiling and sending bits of dust from the plaster falling around us. My elbow caused Ron's grip to loosen on the gun resulting in him dropping it. I turned slightly to see where Laura was and she remained standing behind me confused and shocked.

"Uhh," I let out as one of Ron's fists connected with my ribs, causing me to double over and my own gun spilled out of my waistband. "Laura, run! To the door!" I yelled as I turned my full attention back to Ron. I blocked another incoming fist, this time towards my face. I saw Laura run past us out of the corner of my eye, but my full attention was on Ron. I was on the defensive as he attempted to inflict rain blow after blow on me. I deflected them well enough as I was lighter on my feet than he was, but I knew I needed to apply a little damage of my own to slow him down. On his next swing, I ducked low and moved into his side fast, sending a left hook to his spleen. He howled and doubled over. I was about to send a kick to his groin when I hear...

"Daddy!"

The stampede of Li and the rest of the men with him caught my attention and in those few moments, Ron recovered. Liam's big body entered my line of sight just as Ron grabbed me from behind and tightened his grip around my throat, pressing something hard and sharp to it. I couldn't see it, but I knew it was an Army knife.

"Ron what the fuck are you doing?!" Li's voice bellowed around the room.

I watched the different emotions shine in Liam's eyes. First it was shock, then pure, unfiltered fury when he looked at Ron, and a hint of fear and helplessness when his eyes landed on my neck.

"Yeah, Ron why don't you tell him what you're doing?" I goaded.

"Shut up!" Ron yelled in my ear.

"You've been working with my father this whole time?"

"Look, I was, b-but it wasn't like that. I wasn't involved in drugs, guns or women. I didn't know anything about that."

I felt Ron's spittle hit the side of my face as he tried to defend his actions. His grip on reality quickly fading.

"You told my father. You were the only person I told that I was going to propose. That's how he found and why he threatened Coral and her family." Liam was saying out loud what I too, had realized not that long ago.

"SHE'S NOT RIGHT FOR YOU!" Ron yelled, tightening his grip on my throat.

I felt my airway closing in and knew I need to make my move.

"Daddy what is he doing?!?" A terrified Laura shrilled.

I looked down to see that Laura had somehow moved to the front of Liam, clinging to Liam's leg as she screamed and watched the scene in front of her unfold. The terror in her eyes broke my heart. I wanted to make it better for her. I glanced up to stare at Liam and try to gain his attention, but his gaze was caught between a crying Laura and where Ron held the knife to my throat.

Brian's attempts to grab Laura to get her out of the room led to even louder cries and fighting as Laura grasped tighter onto Liam's leg.

"Why don't you tell him, Ron?" I taunted. "Tell him why you followed him around all these years."

"Shut up!" Ron's voice was hoarse, knowing his secret is going to be exposed soon.

"Why? If I'm not right for him, tell him who is," I goaded.

Finally, Liam looked me in the eye; his eyes filled with questions. I shifted my eyes down to a still hysterical Laura and back up to him and then again before raising my eyebrows.

Realization took hold of Liam and without moving the rest of his body, his hand reached down and covered Laura's eyes, shielding her from what was about to happen. With that done, I knew it was time to wrap this shit up.

Liam's voice was low, deadly, yet filled with an underlying panic as he advised, "You have one more chance to put the fucking knife down if you want to make it out of here alive."

"You would kill me for this b-" he began, and for a second he let his hold on my neck go, pointing the knife wildly in the air.

I didn't give Ron a chance to finish when I sent an elbow to his ribs, gripped the wrist holding the knife, and twisted as hard as I could. Not letting the wrist go, I took a step and pivoted until I was now behind Ron, throwing my free arm around his neck. With his own hand I drove the knife into the center of his back, so deeply I knew I'd punctured his heart. I felt him struggle as the life left his body, but I didn't let go until I heard the ceasing of his gurgling breaths and his heart had stopped beating. When it did I released him and stepped back let his body fall to the floor. I took a deep breath, and looked up to see Liam remove his hand from Laura's eyes to pick her up.

Within two strides Liam was pulling me into him with his free arm and I instantly sunk into him. I didn't even care that his grip was so tight that I felt like I was being crushed. I welcomed this sense of security I'd only felt in his arms. I felt little arms inch their way around my neck and pulled back to see Laura was clinging to me almost as tightly as Liam. I was sure her mind didn't understand what just happened, but she clearly understood I was in danger.

My family. Were the only two words that kept going through my mind. Liam finally let me go and I took Laura into my arms holding her against me so she didn't see Ron's prone body on the floor as we exited the suite.

* * *

Liam

"I don't understand why he did all this." I shook my head, still in a fury as we rode from the FBI field office in San Antonio to the airport. I reached over and grazed my finger over the bandage on Coral's neck. I knew my father had always been a power hungry SOB, so it was not hard to see how he ended up the way he did. But Ron? He was supposed to be my friend.

"He was in love with you."

Those words were like a splash of cold water to a sleeping man. The obvious signs that I had been ignoring or not quite ready to accept. I stared across the dimly lit town car at Coral. My eyes dropped down to her lap where a sleeping Laura rested peacefully. She hadn't left Coral's side since we left the hotel. She even cried and wailed when I tried to take her so Coral could get checked out by the doctor. She'd been sleep for over an hour and every time I tried to reach in to put her down on the seat, she awakened and clung to Coral's arms. I finally gave up, but as Coral snuggled her closer and stroked her hair, I doubt she minded the intrusion.

"Too bad for him," I commented, thinking about Ron. My only regret was ever trusting him in the first place and not being the one who killed him. When I ran in the room and heard Coral yelling for Laura to run and seeing Ron holding a knife to her throat sent a rage through me unlike any other I had ever felt.

Coral's voice was soft, tremulous as she asked, "You think she'll be okay?"

"What?"

"Laura. What she saw today. No kid should see that type of shit. You think she'll be okay?" The love shining in those hazel eyes was evident even in the dark car.

I reached over and stroked Laura's hair and smiled. "She'll be fine." I reached up and stroked Coral's face. "We'll make sure of it." The car finally stopped as those words passed my lips. We'd arrived at the airport.

"Back to Dallas," Coral mumbled as Brian opened her door.

"You haven't told her?" he asked across the car once we're all out.

Coral hoisted Laura up to hold her more comfortably and looked between the two of us.

I smiled. "I was just about to."

"Care to let me in on the little secret?" She cocked an eyebrow. She was so damn sexy when she did that.

"We're not going back to Dallas. We're taking a little family vacation. I think we need a break and with all the shit that is about to hit the fan in the media it's best for us to get away now."

Coral pondered this for a second and surprisingly, she didn't put up any resistance. She simply smiled and said, "Lead the way." Not even asking where our destination was.

I reached around and pulled her close to me by her waist, gave Laura a kiss on top of her head, and led my girls to the jet that would take us away from all this bullshit for a while.

CHAPTER 23

ight Weeks Later
Coral

"Come here."

That deep gravelly voice instantly made my nipples pebble as if we hadn't just finished a round of morning sex an hour ago. It didn't take much to get me revved up these days. And as I looked across the room into those shining green eyes, I knew he already was well aware of what his words were doing to me. I bet he'd done this on purpose. I grabbed my mug of green tea and made my way over to the table where Liam sat in a pair of sweatpants and a plain white t-shirt. Even in this basic outfit he looked delicious. His muscles rippled under the shirt with every move he made. It made me think of the morning session we'd just shared. I was teaching him yoga and somehow our lesson turned into a make out session, which then turned into me on all fours as he plowed into me from behind. *Damn, I'm getting wet just thinking about it.*

"Ah, be careful!" I yelled as he took advantage of my mind wondering and snatched me by the waist down onto his lap, causing a few drops of my tea to spill on his sweatpants.

"I told you to come here. You were taking too long. Reminiscing about the way I fucked you this morning?"

I wanted to smack that cocky ass grin right off his face, but he already knew the truth. "You're too damn arrogant for your own good," I said instead, as he removed the mug from my hand, placing it on the table.

He merely chuckled before leaning up and tickling my neck with his tongue. I sighed in pleasure at the feeling of his warm tongue on me and his hands reaching under my shirt. He made small circles with his hand on my back that sent chills through my body. He pulled back a little. "Where are your rings?"

I opened my eyes, only then realizing I had closed them in the first place. "Um, upstairs," I said, wanting him to continue doing what he was doing.

"Why aren't you wearing them?" I swore this man was obsessed with me wearing those damn rings. Don't get me wrong, I loved the center cut solitaire, flawless diamond and matching band even though I'd spent weeks refusing to wear rings priced close to a million on my finger...every day. But Li wore me down.

After leaving Austin, we ended up flying to Honolulu where Li owned a home and got married a couple days later in a private ceremony attended by only Brian, Jeremy and Laura of course. The three of us remained secluded on his private little getaway for six weeks. We came back home last week and Liam had been mainly working from home, only going into the office a few days due to the raging media madness. Reporters were still camped out in front of Bennett Industries trying to get an interview.

"I wasn't going anywhere today. Everyone in this house knows we're married. No need to wear my rings to ward off potential suitors here," I said, saucily.

"You still haven't told your family," he frowned.

No, I hadn't. Not because I didn't want them to know. Part of me was a little sad they wouldn't get to experience my wedding. I had no regrets about the way Li and I married, but I felt I'd kept my family from so much of my life, that I felt guilty for not including them in this too. I hadn't even told Tasha about us getting married. I knew she and Stacey would be pissed, as would Jabari and Quincy. My aunt and uncle would just be hurt. I sighed.

"You need to tell Quince and Jabari you're no longer working with them too," he continued.

"Who said I'm not working with them anymore?"

"How are you going to continue working with them and run the Community Center as Director?"

I'd already thought of that ever since Brian resigned as director to become Li's new head of security, and Li all but insisted I take on the role. Truthfully, it wasn't much of a fight. I loved that place and I got to bring Laura with me a couple of days a week; it was a win-win. If only I could convince Li to get rid of Mitch following me, but he was not budging on that one. I had twenty-four hour security wherever I went, despite obviously being able to handle myself. I refused to admit I loved how much he looks after me.

"I will work as director at the Community Center here, and maintain a silent partner role in the security company. I'll only help out from a distance when they need it," I answered.

"And when were you planning on telling them? Let me guess," he said cutting off my response, "Soon." He threw out the answer I'd been giving him for two weeks now.

"Soon," I repeated.

He grinned as if he knew something I don't, which he knew I hated. "It's already taken care of," he said cryptically.

Before I could ask what he meant by that, Laura's giggles and Mrs. Mary's laughter interrupted us.

"How do I look?" Laura asked, twirling around. She was dressed in a white fluffy dress, with patent leather shoes and white stockings. Her hair was done in spiral curls and was held back by a flower headband.

I crinkled my brows in confusion. "You look gorgeous, Princess, but what's the occasion?"

I perked up, shocked, as a familiar voice answered. "Your wedding."

"Stacey?" I called just as she rounded the doorway and entered the kitchen.

"Not that you invited us," another familiar voice responded.

"Tasha," I said, as she emerged from behind Stacey.

I just stared at everyone in the room, remaining in Liam's lap in shock. "My wedding?" I finally asked.

I turned my head to look down at Liam and he merely smiled and nodded.

"But we're—"

"Already married. Yeah, we know," Stacey's annoyed voice interjected.

"Thanks for telling us," Tasha said.

I gave Liam a scowl.

"Told you I already handled it," he shrugged.

"We're getting married? Again? In front of my family?" I asked in awe.

Li reached up and cupped my cheek and tilted my head so our foreheads met. "You didn't think I knew you'd want your family to see you get married? I know you better than the back of my own hand." He stroked my cheek lovingly.

Our lips touched and I forgot everyone else in the room.

"I never thought I'd see this damn day. Ol' boy really does have her sprung," a male voice sounded out, interrupting our kiss. I looked up to scowl at Jabari's smart ass.

"I can still kick your a—" I stopped when I saw Laura silently watching me. "Behind," I said turning back to Jabari who stood next to Quincy. Those two with their dark brown skin, tall statures and imposing builds were both a sight to behold. I looked at Quincy's smile and felt a sense of relief knowing he had gotten over his animosity towards Liam. That ever-present sadness still lingered in his eyes, however, and it made my heart ache. We both knew what it was like to lose the love of our lives. I only hoped that one day, Quince would be able to find what I found and heal.

"Enough of that gushy stuff, we only have an hour to get your makeup and hair done and dressed for this ceremony," Stacey rushed as she pulled me from Liam's lap. I looked back at my husband and he was grinning from ear to ear.

"I'll meet you at the aisle, CeCe." Li winked at me.

* * *

CORAL

Where I Sleep. I smiled as the Emeli Sandé song played because this was truly how I felt. This home, with Li and Laura was where I belonged. I pressed my left hand to my belly. This was where I slept. The smile remained frozen on my face as I thought of all the planning Li had gone through to make this day special. Our backyard had been decorated and tents set up for the reception. Bright pink and purple imported flower petals were spread throughout the grounds. He'd even planned our attire. For me, he'd chosen a simple, long white silk dress with a lace shawl, and he wore tuxedo pants and white button up shirt. Very casual, just the way I liked it.

I looked over and saw Liam and Laura playing with Jabari and Quincy. The scene in front of me showed me how much I had truly missed my family over the years.

I turned my head towards the sky and wondered if my mother could see us. "I hope I made you proud, Mama," I said, just above a whisper.

"You've made her more than proud and me too," my Aunt Ruth said behind me.

I turned towards her and felt the usual heartache, staring into her face. She and my mother had been identical twins. Although Stacey was young when our mother died, I was old enough to remember everything about her, down to how she smelled. My aunt with her caramel complexion, chestnut colored eyes and petite frame, stood a couple of inches shorter than me, even in heels. She reminded me so much of my mother. It was another one of the reasons I'd kept my distance all these years. It hurt to look at her, but I was working on moving past that.

"Thank you."

"Thank you for allowing us to come stay with you next week. I can't wait to spend more time with you and that precious little Laura and the one on the way," she smiled and winked at me.

I blinked in shock and my gaze shot over to where Liam was, accusingly.

"He didn't spill your little secret," my aunt said. "The way you can't keep your hand off your stomach for more than a few minutes did." She eyed my hand resting on my still flat stomach.

I immediately pulled my hand away. "I'm not that far along," I confessed, biting the inside of my cheek to suppress a grin. I couldn't help how happy this day and the knowledge of our baby growing in my stomach made me.

"I can't wait to meet him," my Aunt replied.

"Him?" I question.

"Trust me on this. This one will be a boy," she smirked and pulled me into a hug. For the first time in a long time, I actually allowed my aunt to hug me and it felt good.

"I need to go find that uncle of yours and make sure he isn't overindulging on that delicious tiramisu cake." We both laughed at that. My uncle had a huge sweet tooth.

I laughed out loud a few moments later when I saw my aunt scolding my uncle who was indeed holding a plate with another slice of cake.

"I love you."

My whole body reacted to those whispered words in my ear. "Show me," I whispered back and Liam wasted no time cupping my face and pulling me in for a heated kiss. I could no longer feel the ground beneath my feet, only his passion and possession as his tongue swept through my mouth. I moaned, forgetting we were not alone until I heard the clanking of glasses. I pulled back to see our guests tapping their glasses with silverware and applauding us. We both laughed.

"That's just a preview of what's to come later." The promise in his voice sent my belly quaking.

We continued dancing when another slow song came on. Out of

the corner of my eye I saw Jeremy eyeing Tasha like she was a perfectly broiled sirloin. He pulled her onto the dance floor, even though she seemed nervous. Without thinking, I moved towards them only to be stopped by Li.

"Where are you going?"

"Tasha, she…"

"She's just dancing."

"Yeah, with your cousin who is eyeing her the same way you eyed me in those yoga pants this morning. Your cousin is a certified freak with a dark side. Tasha's not ready for that."

Maybe they'd be good for one another. They've both been through a lot," Liam responded.

I merely huffed and continued staring across the dance floor at the pair.

"Li, you know what she's been through," I reminded him.

He nodded. "And I know what he's been through and my cousin would never hurt her or any other woman."

"I know that. I just meant…"

"You're just being your usual overprotective self. Tasha's fine. Come here I want to hold my wife," he pulled me back to him. "But speaking of Tasha, when are you two going to tell Stacey and the rest of your family?"

I rested my head on his strong chest and sighed. "I don't know. Tasha didn't like the idea of me interrupting our wedding day to tell the rest of the family that she's the illegitimate child of my asshole father who cheated on his dying wife."

"She'll let everyone know when she's ready and you'll be there for her just like you've always been," he said, before bending down and pressing a kiss to the corner of my mouth. His hand moved around from my waist to my abdomen. "How's our little guy?"

I shook my head. "Aunt Ruth says it's going to be a boy too."

"I told you it's going to be a boy. Have you eaten enough today? You've been on your feet all day. Want to sit down?" Li began practically pushing me to where the tables and chairs were.

"Li, I'm fine." I swatted his hands away. He'd become even more overprotective since learning I was pregnant. I was nearly ten weeks along.

"I'm just making sure—"

"Daddy! Uncle Jabari's gonna teach me to ride a bike!" an excited Laura ran over to us saying.

Li picked her up kissing her cheek. "We may have to wait on that one, Princess," Liam replied also wrapping his arm around my waist.

As Beyoncé's new song *All Night Long* began playing, Li walked all three of us to the dance floor. I leaned against him and wrapped one arm around him and cupped Laura's cheek with the other. Together all three of us danced to the song in our own little world.

For the first time ever, I felt whole.

* * *

TASHA AND JERMEY'S story coming back soon!

To stay in touch and keep updated on new releases, giveaways and sales, click here to join my newsletter.

www.ingramcontent.com/pod-product-compliance
Lightning Source LLC
Chambersburg PA
CBHW071300190726
48292CB00007B/2628